Praise for David Rosenfelt and the Andy Carpenter Novels

"Fans of legal thrillers and golden retrievers, take heart."
—The Seattle Times

"In each and every book, Rosenfelt manages to make the reading both humorous (laugh-out-loud funny) and edge-of-your-seat suspenseful." *—HuffPost*

"[Rosenfelt] never fails to deliver full value."
—Sullivan County Democrat

"Rosenfelt's mysteries are always delightful reading."
—Jersey's Best

"This long-running series remains as fresh as ever."
—Publishers Weekly

Dog Eat Dog

"Smartly written." *—Red Carpet Crash*

"Fans of brisk, dog-filled mysteries in general [will enjoy *Dog Eat Dog*]." *—Library Journal*

"Rosenfelt has ingeniously created a very suspenseful, highly provocative mystery filled with a vast assortment of characters."
—Gumshoe Review

"Andy is funny, smart, sarcastic, and self-deprecating, and I never fail to laugh out loud while reading these books."
—Rhapsody in Books Weblog

ALSO BY DAVID ROSENFELT

DOG
EAT
DOG

David Rosenfelt

MINOTAUR BOOKS
NEW YORK

Published in the United States by Minotaur Books,
an imprint of St. Martin's Publishing Group

www.minotaurbooks.com

The Library of Congress has cataloged the hardcover edition as follows:

Names: Rosenfelt, David, author.
Title: Dog eat dog / David Rosenfelt.
Description: First Edition. | New York : Minotaur Books, 2021. |
   Series: An Andy Carpenter novel ; 23
Identifiers: LCCN 2021008171 | ISBN 9781250257123 (hardcover) |
   ISBN 9781250257130 (ebook)
Subjects: GSAFD: Mystery fiction. | Suspense fiction.
Classification: LCC PS3618.O838 D63 2021 | DDC 813/.6—dc23
LC record available at https://lccn.loc.gov/2021008171

ISBN 978-1-250-84719-5 (trade paperback)

Our books may be purchased in bulk for promotional, educational,
or business use. Please contact your local bookseller or the Macmillan
Corporate and Premium Sales Department at 1-800-221-7945, extension
5442, or by email at MacmillanSpecialMarkets@macmillan.com.

First Minotaur Books Trade Paperback Edition: 2022

10 9 8 7 6 5 4 3 2 1

The invader picked the wrong house, and it was up to Peter Charkin to make sure that he knew it.

It was an obvious robbery attempt . . . a home invasion. The guy had shown a gun, so Charkin had no choice but to submit to being tied to the chair. He also couldn't prevent the same thing happening to his girlfriend, Tina Welker.

It was Tina's house, which made it a strange choice. Tina was not wealthy, and she lived in a working-class neighborhood. But this was the house the guy had chosen, and Charkin had the misfortune to be there when the robber entered.

The robber was a big guy; the truth is that he was a lot more than Charkin could handle under any circumstances, gun or no gun. But the guy didn't seem as if he intended to hurt anyone, and he had said so up front. He seemed calm, as if he had done this before. No sense antagonizing him.

"Everybody cooperates, and life goes on," the guy had said.

But just to be sure, Charkin had told him he was making a mistake, picking on the wrong people. "You know Jerry Donnelly?" Charkin asked him. "Ever heard of Big Jerry Donnelly?"

The guy had just about done a double take; the Donnelly name was an important one. "What about him?"

"So you know who he is?"

"I know who he is. I said, what about him?"

"He and I are friends. Partners."

"Yeah, right."

"He'll know you did this," Charkin said, before realizing that he had just given the thief a reason to kill him, so as to prevent him from squealing to Donnelly. "I won't tell him, but he'll know."

"You'd better not tell him."

"I won't if you walk away now. There's nothing worth anything here anyway." Charkin winked at the frightened Tina, tied to a chair about six feet away from him. It was his way of telling her that everything would be okay. She did not seem convinced.

"He does know Jerry," Tina said, though she had no idea if that was true and doubted it was. She had never even heard of Donnelly, but that didn't stop her from throwing in her own lie. "And so do I."

The guy looked at her, didn't say anything, and did something that made Charkin think that maybe this wasn't going to end well. The guy punched him in the mouth. Not that hard; the guy could have crushed his face if he wanted to.

Charkin's head went back in the chair. He was stunned by the punch, and by the taste of blood in his mouth. "What did you do that for?" he managed. "We're cooperating."

The assailant didn't answer; instead he quickly took the gun back out of his pocket, put it to Charkin's head, and pulled the trigger. It happened so fast that Charkin did not realize it was coming.

Tina Welker was not so lucky. She experienced the full measure of panic and dread before her life was ended in the same manner as Charkin's.

Then the killer got to work preparing the scene.

The last thing he was worried about was Jerry Donnelly.

We have started taking family dog walks.

Occasionally, usually on the weekends, Laurie, Ricky, and I take Tara and Sebastian for a walk all together. We go from our house on Forty-second Street in Paterson, New Jersey, down to Park Avenue and Thirty-third Street, and then to Eastside Park.

We go to Park Avenue to stop and get bagels and muffins, then we sit and eat them at picnic tables in the park. Tara and Sebastian each get their own plain bagel. Tara, a golden retriever, eats slowly and delicately, while Sebastian, a basset hound, chows his down in about ten seconds. He then looks at Tara, hoping she won't finish.

Good luck with that.

Laurie usually holds Tara's leash. Tara displays a typical golden retriever's interest in her surroundings, eagerly sniffing new discoveries even though she has made this exact walk hundreds of times. Ricky walks Sebastian, and even though Sebastian outweighs him, he has no difficulty handling him. That is because Sebastian walks with the speed and dexterity of your average refrigerator/freezer.

My job, which Laurie and Ricky unanimously assigned to me, is to be the bearer, and user, of the plastic bag. As you can imagine, it is not a job I relish. In Tara's case, it's no big deal; she does her business neatly and delicately.

Sebastian is a different story. Even though he eats the same amount of food as Tara, for some reason there is a clear difference between the input and the output. There are occasions when I could use a forklift to remove Sebastian's "deposits." If he's embarrassed by it, he hides it well.

Today we make a slight detour, stopping on Thirty-ninth Street to drop Ricky off at the house of his best friend, Will Rubenstein. Will's father, Brian, is outside mowing his lawn. My preferred method of lawn mowing is to hire someone. If such people were suddenly to become unavailable, I would choose to cover the whole thing with cement.

With Ricky no longer with us, I take Sebastian's leash and we're back heading to Park Avenue. Sebastian keeps us going at a snail's pace, which is fine with me. He and I share the same point of view: we are going to get there eventually, and neither of us are angling to make the Olympic walking team.

We're one block from the bagel store when I hear a dog yelping, apparently in pain. It's an awful sound, and I quickly look down to make sure it is not coming from Tara or Sebastian. It isn't.

The yelping stops momentarily, but then starts again. Laurie and I look up at the same time, and we see that across and down the street, a man is kicking his dog. The dog is lying on the ground, and the creep is pulling on its leash and kicking it at the same time. He also starts yelling at the dog to get up. The moment is so horrifying that it takes a moment to digest it, to confirm that it's really happening.

Spoiler alert: you are about to learn one of the many differences between Laurie and me.

While we are both horrified, my first reaction is to figure out what to do. Laurie's first reaction is to do it.

She drops Tara's leash and runs across the street toward the creep, yelling at him to stop. He looks at her with what seems to be disdain. He is not aware that she spent years as a cop and could likely handle three of him with ease. Therefore, he is also not aware that if he doesn't stop what he's doing, he's going to get his ass kicked.

I grab Tara's leash, and the two dogs and I belatedly start to move toward the action as well. But then I hear more yelling; a different man's voice this time, and I see another guy running toward the creep and his dog. He is also yelling at him to stop, but it is falling on deaf ears.

The other man, clearly a hero, is closer and arrives before Laurie. The creep drops the leash, whirls, and throws a punch at the arriving hero, which proves to be a major mistake.

The hero proceeds to dismantle the creep with a series of punches. By my count there are at least six of them, evenly distributed between the gut and the head. If you really want to know how fast and crisp the punches look, go on YouTube and check out some Muhammad Ali fights.

The creep goes down as if shot. Laurie yells at the hero to stop hitting the creep, but it's unnecessary, since he's already stopped. He's not leaning over to hit the guy again, though the creep deserves it. All the hero is doing is picking up the dog's leash.

I can't hear what he and Laurie are saying to each other until I get close. The first thing I hear is the guy saying, "I can't stand when people hurt a dog."

The dog at the center of this, an adorable pug, has gotten to his feet and seems none the worse for wear. Though his owner is still on the ground, the pug makes no effort to go over to him. I don't blame the dog.

I see other people watching from across the street. I assume one or more of them called 911, because sirens are blaring as police cars approach. I am surprised to see a look of concern, if not panic, in the man's eyes; as a defense attorney, I have seen the look before.

"Don't worry," I say. "It was self-defense. We both saw it."

"You don't understand," he says, in a voice that I can only describe as resigned. The police have pulled up and are approaching, so that is the extent of our conversation.

The creep on the ground has come to and is slowly getting to his feet. The cops put handcuffs on both men, no doubt until they can sort things out. The hero who won the fight hands me the pug's leash just before they cuff him. The pug seems fine with that; as long as it's not getting kicked anymore, the dog is good with the situation.

Fortunately, Laurie knows the cop who seems to be in charge. This is not unusual, as she was a lieutenant in the Paterson PD for a number of years before leaving and becoming an investigator for me. She also taught for a while at the Academy, so a lot of these officers remember her.

She goes over and talks to the cop. . . . I can hear her refer to him as John. They speak for a while, then she comes back to me. "They're going to take them both into custody for now."

"It was self-defense."

"I told him that. I also said we'd sign statements. Meanwhile, we should take the dog."

I walk over to the hero. "I'm a lawyer. My name is Andy Carpenter. I'll make sure this goes well for you."

"It won't."

It's a strange comment; I'm not sure why he is so negative

about the situation. "Trust me. You did the right thing. You prevented dog abuse, and the asshole threw the first punch."

He just shakes his head. "Doesn't matter."

"What's your name?"

"Matt. Matt Jantzen. Will you take care of the dog?"

"Absolutely." I take out my card and hand it to him. "Call me if you need help."

You think I should go down there?" I ask Laurie when we get home. We aborted the walk and didn't stop for the bagels.

"The police station?"

"Yes."

"Why would you do that?"

"To make sure he's okay. I'm an eyewitness to the event."

"You're also a lawyer. Now you're hunting for clients?"

The irony of this is not escaping Laurie. With more than enough money to retire as the result of a huge inheritance several years ago and some lucrative cases, and more than enough dislike for lawyering, I've been trying to avoid taking on clients for a number of years. That I'm rarely successful in that avoidance has not deterred me from continuing to try.

"You know better than that," I say. "But since I'm already involved . . ."

She smiles. "And since he did what he did to protect a dog . . ."

She's got me. "Guilty as charged. Besides, there was something about his attitude that was weird."

"What does that mean?"

"I'm not sure. He said that things were not going to go well, but it wasn't like he was worried. It was more like he was resigned to it."

"Maybe he's gotten into street fights before. And maybe the other times he started them."

"He certainly knew how to handle himself. So you think I should go?"

"You gave him your card. I would imagine he'll call you if he needs you. Or he can just dial 1–800-I'M RETIRED."

I nod. "Okay, you're right. The last thing I need to do is inject myself into this situation." I point to the pug that we brought home with us. He is sleeping on a dog bed with Tara, looking like he's lived here all his life. "What should we do with him?"

Laurie shrugs. "Let him sleep. But we'll have to make a decision on what to do if his owner tries to get him back."

"Come on, you know I've already made that decision, and so have you. We are not sending him back to get kicked again. That is a nonstarter; this dog is one client I would happily defend."

I go over and look at his tag; I hadn't thought to do that before. "His name is Hunter. He doesn't look much like a hunter."

Laurie smiles, leans over, and pets the sleeping, very comfortable dog. "Welcome, Hunter. Make yourself at home."

Since we never got our bagels, I head back out to get some. I drive this time, which is my preference anyway. I get there faster, with little effort, and I don't have to keep bending over to pick up dog shit.

Just as I'm just leaving the store, my cell phone rings. "Pete Stanton called. Matt Jantzen told him that you were his attorney," Laurie says.

"Why?"

"I guess because you gave him your card, told him you were an attorney, and offered to help. Nice gestures have consequences, Andy."

"No, I mean, why Pete?" Pete Stanton is a close friend, and the only officer on the entire Paterson police force that doesn't hate me 100 percent of the time. Pete is a 50 percenter in that regard. But he's also the captain of the Homicide Division; I have no idea why he would be involved in a street-fight case like this one.

"I don't know," she says. "Maybe he was walking by and heard that they were trying to reach you. But then again, there might be more going on."

"Why do you say that?"

"Pete said they are transferring Jantzen to the jail, and that you should head down there."

"Could the creep who was kicking the dog have died? Maybe the punches jarred his tiny brain loose, or something."

"You'll find out soon enough, should you decide to go."

"You know I'm going to go."

I head straight down to the jail, which is about twenty minutes away. I take the bagels with me; I think Laurie and I might wind up having them for dinner. Special parking spaces are assigned to lawyers, and even though it pains me to think of myself as a lawyer, I'm not above taking one.

I've been here far too many times, but at least I know my way around, and I certainly know the cops who work here. They don't like me, of course, because I am a defense attorney and a particularly obnoxious one at that. But they know that if they give me a hard time, I'll file enough complaints to make their lives miserable. So they treat me professionally, with just a little snarling thrown in.

I ask the guy at the desk if Pete Stanton is around and he says, "No."

That seems to resolve that issue, so I ask to see Matt Jantzen. I'm already listed as his attorney, and they seem to be expecting me, so it only takes a half hour to arrange the meeting. That is warp speed in jail time.

Jantzen is brought into the meeting room, already in prison garb and handcuffed. This seems like overkill for his street fight; clearly, something else is going on.

"Thanks for coming. I'm sorry to drag you into this, but I didn't know who else to turn to. I'm not from around here."

"Have you been arrested and booked?" I ask, though the answer is obvious.

He nods. "Yes."

"For assault?"

"No. Murder."

"The guy with the dog? Did he die?"

"No. Someone else. Two people, actually. Back in Maine. They ran my identification and it popped up that I was wanted. I knew it would. I guess it's not important to say it at this stage, but I am innocent of the charge."

"Is Maine home?"

"That's a bit of a story. It used to be home, and it was going to be home again, before this all started. But that doesn't seem very important now. They're talking about extraditing me. I didn't know how to deal with that, which is why I asked them to call you. I'm sorry about that."

"Don't worry about it. I volunteered because of how you protected that dog."

"It was an instinct."

"A good one. I'll deal with the extradition request, but there's no upside to your contesting it. It's basically a formality; New Jersey will go along with it whether you fight it or not. Maine is making the request, not Yemen."

He nods. "That's what I figured. Thanks."

"Do you have a criminal attorney in Maine?"

"No." He shrugs. "I've gone my whole life without needing one."

"I'll see if I can get a recommendation. You have money to pay legal fees?"

"Yours?"

"No, I mean in Maine."

He shakes his head. "No chance."

"That may lessen the number of lawyers who want to take your case to somewhere in the zero range. Who are you alleged to have murdered?"

"Two people, a man and a woman. The guy is named Peter Charkin and the woman is Tina Welker. They were killed two years ago."

"What was your relationship to them?"

"I didn't have any. I never met either of them. I vaguely remember the murders, but I don't think I ever knew their names until my sister told me about them."

"How did your sister know about it?"

He shrugs. "It was all over the news back then. But I don't have any idea if she knows any more than was public knowledge. I doubt it, but I never asked her. I've only known my sister for a few weeks."

I was thinking maybe I should go up to Maine," I say.

Laurie smiles an irritating, knowing smile. "Is that what you were thinking?"

"Yes. I haven't been away in a while and I've always wanted to see the White Mountains."

"The White Mountains are in New Hampshire."

I nod. "I know that, but you can see them from Maine. They're mountains, so they're really high. And if there's an avalanche, I'd be at a safe distance."

"An avalanche in June?"

I nod. "You can never be too careful."

"What's going on here, Andy? You're going to take on a murder case in Maine? You spend all your time trying to avoid them in New Jersey . . . and you live in New Jersey."

"I'm not taking on a case; I'm just going to help this guy get set up with adequate counsel and make sure he's well taken care of. I feel like I owe him that. But if you don't want me to . . ."

"You know I'm in favor of you doing whatever you want; I'm just trying to understand what's behind it. Usually you have to be dragged kicking and screaming into a case."

"Fair enough. I've been thinking about exactly that, doing some introspection."

Her face reflects her surprise. "You've been doing introspection? You're better at ballet than introspection."

"I'll admit it's not my specialty, but hear me out. I asked Jantzen why he did what he did, knowing that it could draw the police and put himself in jeopardy. He basically said it was an instinct, that he saw the dog needed help and he just reacted."

Laurie nods. "I can understand that. I had the same instinct."

"Right. So I shudder to say this, but maybe I have a lawyer instinct. This guy needs help, and as a defense attorney I'm in a position to provide that help."

She smiles. "Andy Carpenter admitting to a lawyer's instinct. There's never a tape recorder around when you need one."

"This introspection is a dangerous thing. I don't recommend it; I much prefer ballet."

"When are you going?"

"I should go right away. Are you going to be okay without me here? Everything will fall on you."

"Well, with you gone, I'll have to bring someone in to watch baseball."

"Come on, I do more than that."

"You mean basketball?" Then, "Andy, you know I'm kidding. I think helping Jantzen is a noble thing to do, and you're by far the best person to do it. Unless he's a double murderer."

I nod. "Which is a definite possibility."

"You know very little about his case."

"I really know nothing about it; I didn't want to press him on it. It's not like I'm his lawyer."

"All evidence to the contrary. You going to take Tara with you?"

I shake my head. "No, I won't be there long enough. I've already started making some calls to people to see if they can recommend local counsel. I'd wind up leaving her in a hotel, and that's not fair. She's better off here."

"Where in Maine is this?"

"The arraignment is going to take place in a town called Wiscasset, which is in an area that they call the Midcoast. I think that's because it's midway up in the state and near the coast."

"Makes sense."

I nod. "That does, but north of Midcoast is Down East. For some reason they must think you're going down when you go north. Anyway, it's about seven hours from here, so I'll just drive up. I'll be back before you can say, 'Damn, I really miss Andy.'"

I knew Laurie would be supportive; she thinks I'm a lawyer at heart and that I need to be practicing my craft. But the truth is that I'm not looking forward to this. I'm going to miss her and Ricky and Tara and even Sebastian.

Had this taken place two weeks from now, the timing would have been perfect. Ricky will be going back to the camp he attended last summer, which is in Maine. We could have dropped him off and Laurie could have stayed with me while I was there; it could have been a mini-vacation, except for the lawyer-work part.

I'm hoping to be gone only for a few days, but the amount of time I am going to be away never influences how I pack. Basically I just throw all of my clothes into one or two suitcases; I can make decisions on what to wear when I get there.

One conscious decision I make is to only bring one suit. It's my way of vowing to myself that if I get into court at all, it will only be once or twice. This trip is going to be of limited duration.

I call the jail and ask to speak to my client, though I hate using that word. He's unavailable, but calls me back in thirty-five minutes. I tell him that I will meet him in Maine, and that he is not to talk about the case with anyone.

"I deeply appreciate this," he says. "I read about you online; they let me have an hour today on a computer."

"I'm online?"

"Are you kidding? You have your own Wikipedia page; you're a famous lawyer."

"Don't believe everything you read."

"It also says you love dogs, and that you rescue them. That's why you're doing this, right? Because I helped a dog?"

"Maybe you can believe everything you read."

Preparing to leave is not exactly time-consuming for me.

Since I do little around here, I don't have to get people to cover for me. If a lawyer has no clients to represent in the forest, does he make a sound?

I call Willie Miller, my former client who is my partner in the Tara Foundation, which rescues dogs and finds them homes. He and his wife, Sondra, essentially run the foundation. I stop off occasionally to play with the dogs, but I basically get in the way. So when I tell Willie I'll be gone for a few days, he doesn't exactly panic.

I don't have to alert the other members of our legal team because we don't currently have any clients. And Pete Stanton and Vince Sanders, the two friends who I share a regular table with at Charlie's Sports bar/restaurant, won't even notice I'm not there. If I stopped paying the tab that we collectively run up, they would notice and freak out. Someday I have to try that.

Saying good-bye to Laurie and Ricky is tough, even though it's for such a brief period. We are almost never separated, and I'm going to miss them.

Tara is also a tough one, but a biscuit seems to ease the pain for her. Sebastian doesn't consider my departure important enough to wake up for, so I tell Tara to convey my good-byes to him when he gets up. He normally awakens at mealtime and stays awake for the duration of the meal. Hunter doesn't know me well enough to care one way or the other, but since he's started emulating Tara, he seems fine with a biscuit as well.

My GPS tells me that the trip is going to take six hours and eighteen minutes. I do whatever the GPS tells me, blindly and without questioning.

I still find it amazing that a woman's voice (I call her Shirley) is in my car with me, telling me where to turn. That said, our relationship is not perfect. She occasionally gets annoyed at me if I don't perfectly follow her instructions, and I get pissed when I don't think she is doing her job correctly.

I have to confess that at times I've raised my voice at her ("WHAT DO YOU MEAN, 'BEAR RIGHT,' SHIRLEY? IT'S EITHER A RIGHT TURN OR IT ISN'T! I'M LOOKING AT IT FROM HERE ON THE GROUND, AND 'BEARING' IS NOT AN OPTION!")

But we work it out, and the positives in our relationship far outweigh the negatives. She has some great traits. For example, she doesn't mind if I listen to sports on the radio, and she never has to stop to go to the bathroom. Best of all, she pretty much stays focused on getting me where I want to go, and I can respect that.

With Shirley handling the navigating, I have plenty of time to think about the little I've learned about Jantzen's case so far. Whatever I know comes from googling stories in the *Portland Press Herald;* most of them were from the time of the murders, but there have been a few updates announcing Jantzen's arrest.

Peter Charkin and Tina Welker were found dead in Welker's home in Nobleboro, Maine, a little more than two years ago. Police at the time said that it appeared to be a home invasion; both victims were bound and then shot, execution-style. The house was ransacked, but there was no mention of what might have been taken. Of course, the police would have no way of even knowing that, since they would not have definitive knowledge of what was there in the first place.

Charkin apparently put up a struggle, but was subdued. There is no explanation of specifics, but DNA that belonged to neither Charkin nor Welker was found at the scene.

Since a typical house contains DNA from many people, I can only assume that this particular DNA was somehow tied to the murder. Maybe it was derived from scratched skin under the victim's fingernails or blood unconnected to the victims. There are certainly other possibilities as well.

Current stories are about Jantzen's arrest in New Jersey and his imminent extradition to Maine. He is said to have recently moved to Damariscotta, about ten minutes from the murder scene, but no information has come forward linking Jantzen to either of the victims prior to their deaths.

Based on just the coverage in Portland, which is more than an hour from Damariscotta, this murder case seems to have been a big deal.

While this week's stories report that DNA evidence is what tied Jantzen to the murders, how the connection was suddenly made two years after the event is not explained. The state police in Maine are not giving out much information, but profess confidence that they have their man.

"They've got DNA, Shirley. That's never a good sign."

She doesn't respond, probably considering the implications of what I've said. A minute goes by and then she says, "Heavy traffic up ahead."

I don't know if she means that as a metaphor for the case, but I find out soon enough. The traffic I hit is pretty bad, and it's a good eight hours before I arrive at my destination, the Cod

Cove Inn, located in Edgecomb. On the way, I drive through Wiscasset and past the courthouse where the arraignment is to take place; it's then another fifteen minutes to the inn.

It shouldn't even take that long, but a huge line of people gathered to buy lobster rolls at a little shack called Red's Eats causes a traffic backup. A lobster roll place across the street from Red's has hardly any customers; I'm not sure why there is such a disparity. A lobster, it would seem to me, is a lobster. And a roll is definitely a roll.

Laurie found the Cod Cove Inn online and said it looked good. She was right; it's perfect for what I need. It's unlike what I picture in a small-town inn; it has running water, an elevator, stairs that don't creak, comfortable large rooms, and working telephones. It's more of a hotel than an inn.

Most important, it has televisions in the rooms! With cable! And ESPN! Had the Pilgrims been smart, they would have left Plymouth Rock and come up here.

While they do serve a continental breakfast, the smiling woman behind the desk regretfully informs me that they don't have a restaurant. So I head back to Wiscasset to get a lobster roll. Rather than wait on the huge line at Red's, I go to the place across the street to get what turns out to be a delicious one. I notice that the woman across from me wears a sweatshirt that says I ROOT FOR TWO TEAMS. THE RED SOX, AND WHOEVER IS PLAYING THE YANKEES.

After eating, I head back to the inn to call Laurie and make sure everything is okay at home. I'm tired from the drive and will no doubt fall asleep to the blissful sounds of an ESPN baseball game.

Tomorrow I have to get back to the real legal world.

You came all the way from New York to ask me that?"

That is the less than encouraging response I get from Charlie Tilton. Tilton is a criminal attorney in Damariscotta, a town near Wiscasset. I've been up here before while working on a previous case, so I know my way around fairly well.

I had gotten Tilton's name from Tim Haskins, a lawyer friend of mine who has a summer house not far from here. Tim's a civil attorney, so not suitable for this job, but he recommended Tilton, who agreed to see me first thing this morning.

"Actually, I came from New Jersey."

"Same thing. You a Yankees fan?"

I shake my head and answer truthfully. "Nope . . . can't stand them. Mets all the way."

He looks at me strangely, as if trying to determine whether I am telling the truth, or what I think he wants to hear. "Okay," he finally says. "You want some coffee?"

"You don't offer coffee to Yankee fans?"

"I do, but you don't want to know what I put in it."

I accept his offer for coffee, and once we're settled, I reask the question. "So, how would you feel about representing Matt Jantzen?"

"I know it's only nine o'clock in the morning, but I'm betting this is the worst offer I get all day."

That response doesn't fill me with optimism. "Because he has no money to pay you?"

"He has no money? Now it is officially the worst offer I will get this decade. But it's not about money."

"So what is it?"

"The killer tied up two people, put a gun to their heads, and pulled the trigger. I know we're just a small town with small-town sensibilities, but that bothered some of the locals. Another way to put it is that it scared the shit out of everybody. Besides that, his DNA ties him to the crime."

"Jantzen says he's innocent."

"He does? Then just tell that to the judge, and he'll be free to go. Judges around here are really trusting that way."

"So you don't subscribe to the 'everybody deserves a good defense' principle?"

"My subscription ran out and I forgot to renew." Then, "Come on, you're a big-time lawyer; I read about you online when you called to set up this meeting. You're hot shit."

I nod. "I am, in fact, hot shit. But that is not exactly on point here."

"Why not? You're going to do everything; you just need some local dope to sit next to you. You want me to be that dope."

He's referring to how an out-of-state attorney needs local counsel to provide cover for him to operate in the courtroom. The out-of-state person needs to get what is called pro hac vice, which is essentially a formality that allows him to practice there that one time.

The local counsel is basically just vouching for the out-of-state attorney. It's not essential for the local person to actually participate in the trial, but judges usually prefer when they do. Lawyers usually like to do what judges prefer.

"You're the dope that was recommended by Tim Haskins, who also mentioned something about you owing him one. I told Tim that I wouldn't bring that up, so I'm not going to. I'm a man of my word, in addition to being hot shit."

"You're not going to bring up the thing you just brought up?"

"Correct. It would be unseemly to mention that years ago he used connections to get a marijuana possession charge against you dropped that could have impacted your legal career."

"You sure you're not a Yankees fan?"

"Positive. But I think you're missing the point here. I'm not looking for someone to sit next to me during the trial, since I'm going to be back in New Jersey rooting for the Mets."

"You're not trying the case?" he asks, not attempting to mask his surprise.

"No. I got involved due to an unusual circumstance, so I'm just trying to help him out. Then I'm going home to a nonthriving practice and a life of leisure."

"So you're looking for me to be the lawyer of record? The guy that would actually try the case?"

"That pretty much sums it up, yes."

"Just when I think the offer can't get any worse, you raise the bar."

"I'm starting to think you're not going to jump at this."

"Look. You seem like a nice guy, and you hate the Yankees, so I'm going to be straight with you. You are not going to find a lawyer willing to take on a very unpopular client, a case that is probably unwinnable, for no money. Law schools do not turn out such people; you should focus on insane asylum graduates."

I'm not surprised to hear any of this; I knew it was a long

shot. My hope was that a lawyer would want to take on the case simply because it will generate local publicity. I needed to find someone who believed in the "any publicity is good publicity" maxim.

"Tell me about the Public Defender's office here," I say.

"Good, hardworking young lawyers working in an under-staffed, underfunded office. They wouldn't have a chance with this case. Hell, you wouldn't have a chance."

"This is not going as well as I hoped."

Tilton surprises me by laughing out loud. "No, I guess it isn't. I'll tell you what I'll do. I'll set you up with the pro hac vice and then sit with you during the arraignment. Meanwhile, you find another lawyer or take it to the public defender, and then we both ride off into the sunset. That work?"

I nod. "Works for now, thanks." Then, "How 'bout them Red Sox?"

Charlie Tilton and I head down to the courthouse.

Applying for the pro hac vice is a quick, relatively painless procedure. We each fill out a form and submit it to the court clerk. There's little doubt that it will be approved, though I'd probably be better off if it isn't. Then I could get out of here with a clean conscience.

While we're there, we check on the status of Matt Jantzen's extradition and learn that he is due in Maine late this afternoon. They are moving fast.

Before Charlie and I go our separate ways, I ask him if there are any lawyers he could recommend.

"Come on, Andy . . . these guys are my friends."

I'm sure this is going to wind up with the public defender, but I'm not in the mood to deal with that now. What I am in the mood to do is stop for another lobster roll, then go back to my room and take a nap. Getting nowhere is tiring.

Once I get back to the inn, I call Laurie to make sure everything is okay at home and update her on progress here. Obviously the progress report doesn't take a lot of time.

"So how long do you think you'll be there?"

"Two days, three at the outside. Tomorrow is the arraignment;

I'm going to see Jantzen in the morning and then deal with that. I'll work on turning it over to the public defender in the afternoon; hopefully I can get that wrapped up quickly."

"You've been eating okay?"

"I had a lobster roll for dinner last night, a lobster roll for lunch today, and I may grab a couple of lobster rolls for dinner tonight."

"Sounds like a balanced diet."

We talk a little more; mostly it's her telling me that everything is fine at home. I'm feeling guilty that I'm not there, although Laurie is more than capable of picking up the slack. Since I do little other than walk the dogs, there isn't that much slack to pick up.

It's raining, which influences my dinner plans. I'm not going to go back to my outdoor lobster roll place, so I head into Damariscotta. Last time I was here I ate at a terrific restaurant/pub called King Eider's, so I try it again.

It hasn't changed a bit, still has great atmosphere and delicious food. The place is crowded, so I sit and eat at the bar, watching the Red Sox game on the overhead television.

There is some talk about the game, though not as much as I would have thought. That's because a more intriguing topic is on the table, or actually on the bar, and that is the arrest of Matt Jantzen.

The talk ranges from a rehash of the murders themselves, to their having finally made an arrest, to a possible motive, and how the accused has himself a big-shot lawyer from New York City.

The inability of these people to distinguish northern New Jersey from New York is somewhat inexplicable, but apparently widespread. Believe me, people who live in New York and New Jersey definitely know the difference.

One thing that does not come up in the bar conversation is the possibility that Jantzen might be innocent. People refer to the police as having "caught the guy that did it," and the speculation is about what his sentence will be.

They seem to be nice enough people, and one guy who seems more intent on the baseball game than the murder case even offers to buy me a drink. But they are absolutely positive that Jantzen is guilty without having any apparent knowledge about the actual case.

It pains me to say it, but I must have defense attorney blood coursing through my semiretired veins, because it's annoying me. One thing is for sure: getting an impartial jury is not going to be a picnic.

Glad I don't have to worry about it.

I've finished dinner, so I have some coffee and settle in to watch the end of the game. The guy who offered me the drink asks me whether I live around here and I say, "No, I'm a hotshot lawyer from New York."

The word gets around at bar speed, which is 30 percent faster than warp speed. Rather than its generating any ill will, everyone seems intrigued and asks me about the case. They all suddenly profess open-mindedness, which is a cross between their just being nice and total horseshit. If Derek Jeter showed up here, they would claim to be Yankees fans.

I wind up having a pretty good time. These are good people to drink and watch sports with, but I still wouldn't want them on my jury.

As I'm leaving, I'm approached by the man who has been manning the reception desk. He identifies himself as Jed Weiss, one of the owners, and says, "Thanks for coming in."

"Good food, good company, and I'm okay with the Red Sox winning."

He smiles, but the smile quickly fades. "I knew Matt Jantzen when he lived here; we went to high school together."

I don't say anything because it's clear Jed has more to say, and I'm not sure where this is going.

"There is no way that the Matt Jantzen I knew put a gun to anyone's head."

"Thanks. Good to hear."

"He's the kind of guy that if he saw something like that happening, he'd try to stop it."

I nod. "Thanks. I actually already knew that."

Matt Jantzen looks none the worse for wear from his extradition trip to Maine.

Obviously he wasn't taken from New Jersey to Maine on a forced march and, not surprisingly, has been treated reasonably well. Based on what I've seen so far of this place, he's probably been sucking down prison lobster rolls.

We meet in an anteroom in the Wiscasset courthouse. It's the main courthouse for Lincoln County and looks very much like a church. It was built in the early 1800s, which probably makes it one of the newer buildings around here. When locals refer to a building as "prewar," they're talking War of 1812.

"I'm amazed that you're here," Jantzen says.

"Join the club."

"What happens now?"

"Well, in the short term, you're going to be arraigned and charged with these crimes. Your only role is to plead guilty or not guilty. If it's not guilty, a tentative trial date will be set."

"And in the meantime I'll be in jail?"

I nod. "No question about it. I'll ask for it, but based on the nature of the crimes, you have no shot at bail. You'll also be considered a flight risk, since they believe you've been on the run since the murders."

He nods sadly. "I figured that."

"So since we have no control over that, let's focus on what we can control . . . your plea."

"I'm not guilty."

"Is that how you will plead? Taking this to trial would obviously remove the chance of negotiating a lighter sentence, although I am just speculating as to whether that would even be possible. The prosecution's willingness to deal would depend on the strength of their case, and they have not produced any discovery yet."

"I understand."

"Even if you plead not guilty, that doesn't remove the possibility of making a pretrial deal later, if that's the way you ultimately want to go."

He shakes his head firmly. "I'm not interested in a deal. I'm not guilty and I won't say that I am. No matter what."

I nod. "Fair enough. When they ask you to plead, just say, 'Not guilty, Your Honor.' Say it just like you just said it to me."

"Have you learned anything about their evidence?"

"No. But I honestly have no reason to. I've been straight with you; this is as far as I go."

He nods his understanding. "How should I go about getting a lawyer?"

"I've attempted to jump-start that process already, but it's not going to be easy. Representing the accused in a case like this is inherently not terribly popular, but there are usually lawyers willing to do it. When you add your inability to pay their fee into the mix, the attitude changes."

"So it's the public defender?"

"That's my first stop when I leave here."

The bailiff comes in to tell us that the arraignment is ready to begin. We go out to the courtroom, and I'm surprised to see a fairly large crowd in the gallery; it's a good-sized room and is maybe two-thirds full. This is an important case here; I'm afraid that the community has waited a long time to get their revenge on whoever the killer might be. Now they have a name and face to put to it.

The judge, Denise Pressley, comes in and takes her seat. The prosecution team is present in force: four lawyers. I only learn the name of the lead prosecutor when the judge refers to him as Mr. Steinkamp.

As promised, Charlie Tilton is at the defense table waiting for us. We agreed that he will handle the details, after first informing the judge that we are both the attorneys of record for this hearing only. She doesn't question the arrangement.

Things go according to form, and Jantzen delivers his not guilty plea as I advised, firmly and with conviction. We request bail, which is denied, and a trial date is set. It's probably way too soon, especially since the defendant doesn't even have counsel yet, but the date can be changed later on, by his actual lawyer.

When the hearing is gaveled to a close, Jantzen shakes our hands and thanks us. "Will I see either of you again?"

We both hesitate in our answers.

He nods. "That's what I figured. But I appreciate what you've done for me."

knew it was too early for Christmas," Joel York says. "Just last night I said to my wife, 'It's too early for Christmas.'"

York is the director of the Public Defender's office in Lincoln County, and he's reacting to my having just told him that his agency's services will be needed to defend Matt Jantzen.

"I'm impressed with your knowledge of the holiday calendar," I say.

"Thanks. When I first learned that they arrested somebody for the murders, I was upset, you know? I mean, if the guy is really guilty, then I'm glad they caught him, because the murders were terrible, just terrible.

"But I don't have to tell you that arrests mean clients, and clients are something we don't need more of. We've got plenty of clients, but lawyers? Not so many. And money? Even less. But then I heard you were taking the case, and it felt like Christmas. But down deep I knew it was too early for Christmas. I even said so to my wife."

"It's uncanny; and here I thought Christmas was next week. But you, and your wife, knew better. Now, can we talk about Matt Jantzen?"

York frowns. "If we have to."

"He's going to take this to trial; at least that's his current plan.

He has no money to hire a private lawyer, so I took him through the arraignment, and I am assisting him in finding counsel. Which brings me to you."

"It's a stone-cold loser. I'm told they have DNA . . . blood on the scene. What's he claiming, that he showed up, bled for a while, but had nothing to do with the murders?"

I'm not happy with York's attitude, even though he is being honest and is probably correct. A defense attorney who decides in advance that his case is a "stone-cold loser" is unlikely to snatch victory from the jaws of defeat.

"I generally like to hear both sides before I judge guilt or innocence."

"I'm happy for you," he says. "So do I. And we'll handle the case professionally; if he goes down, it won't be because of bad lawyering. But we don't exactly have the funding to conduct full-scale investigations, you know? So if there's another side to this story, it better not be buried too deep."

It's not exactly a situation unique to Lincoln County, Maine. Public defenders never have enough staff or funding to do all that they could do. For the most part they are good, dedicated lawyers carrying their caseloads uphill. I don't know if that is also true for York's department, but I'm betting that it is.

"The case is yours," I say. "If there is a line of investigation that is promising but requires money, call me."

"You'll put money up for this?" he asks, not masking his surprise.

"If it could make the difference, yes."

"I'm impressed."

"Just please give this your best shot; he's in your hands."

"I knew it was too early for Christmas. I even said it to my wife."

I leave York's office feeling uneasy. I can't escape the feeling that I'm abandoning Jantzen to a life sentence, although intellectually I know he is not mine to abandon.

Since I don't have Tara to talk to on our nightly walk, I talk to myself while driving in the car. "It's ridiculous for me to feel guilty. I've already done more than any other lawyer in my position would have done. If we hadn't gone for those damn bagels, I wouldn't even be here."

Tara is not there to answer, so I'm met by silence. I'm used to that since she never answers even when she's with me. She's a dog and therefore does not talk, yet it somehow always makes me feel better when she's there to listen.

I head back to the hotel to call Laurie. It's a brief conversation since I'm not in a talkative mood and because she's busy. Ricky has two friends over and she's trying to prevent them from destroying the house. I've been there; it's an uphill struggle.

I give her a brief rundown on what has transpired, then I tell her that I'll be home tomorrow.

"You sure about this?" she asks.

"I'm sure."

"No regrets if and when you read that he's been convicted?"

"No regrets. I'm sure the public defender is good; he knows the holiday calendar like the back of his hand."

I turn on the local news and there is a story about the arraignment and status of the case. The reporter accurately says that I am resigning from representing Jantzen, though the clear implication is that I am bailing out. Certainly there is no recognition that this was the plan all along.

It's a negative for the public, which includes the jury pool, to get the idea that Jantzen's lawyer is abandoning him. A natural inference would be that I don't want to represent such a client, perhaps because he is a double murderer.

When I am feeling this crummy, I generally try to drown my

sorrows in lobster. So I head back to King Eider's, both for the food and because the Red Sox are playing the Yankees tonight. It should make for an interesting dynamic.

When I get there, Jed Weiss is again at the main desk. "Somebody is here to see you." He points to a table across the room.

A young woman is sitting there alone; is it possible that the big-shot, big-city lawyer has already acquired a Maine groupie? Alas, I doubt it.

"Who is she?"

"I'll let her tell you. But she's a nice lady."

I nod. "What's the score of the game?"

"Two–nothing, Red Sox, top of the second."

"So everyone is happy?"

He frowns. "It's a mixed blessing. We sell more beer when they lose."

Hello, Mr. Carpenter. I'm sorry to intrude on your dinner, but I would appreciate it if we could talk."

She is pleasant looking, maybe in her late twenties, but with a weariness that speaks to a less-than-easy life. She has a nice smile, which she uses on me to good effect, but this is no groupie.

Someday I really want a groupie, just so I can tell Laurie I have one. Although . . . is it possible to have just one? Doesn't a groupie by definition have to be part of a group? These are the kind of questions that haunt me.

"How did you know I'd be here?"

"People who come here have a tendency to return. And I know you were here last night." She shrugs. "It's a small town."

I sit down across from her. "You have the floor. Or the table."

She nods. "My name is Mary Patrick; people call me Mary Pat. I am Matt Jantzen's half sister. I saw him today, and first of all I want to thank you for what you've done for him so far."

The words "so far" are not lost on me; as a shrewd conversation analyst, I know where this is going.

She continues, "I feel like I'm to blame for his predicament."

"How is that?"

"Well, let me start at the beginning. About six weeks ago I

got a phone call from Matt; I had never spoken to him in my life. Until his call, I did not even know he existed.

"He had sent his DNA into one of those ancestry services to try and see if it could turn up any family that he wasn't aware of. His father, who it turns out was also my father, didn't stay in any one place for very long. Anyway, that's how he got my name; I had used the same service a couple of years ago.

"He came here to see me, and it was quite wonderful. We found out that we had many of the same likes and dislikes, personality traits, that kind of thing. It was a long time since I had any warm feelings toward my father, but in a way I was grateful to him for giving me Matt.

"Then a few weeks ago, the police came to the house looking for him. I knew where he was; he was up in Acadia doing some hiking and fishing. But I didn't tell them that because I remembered something."

"What was that?"

"A few months after I sent in my DNA to that service, the state police came by asking questions about where I was back around the time the murders were committed. I don't think they thought I did it, and I couldn't have, because I was away at school in Delaware. But they asked me if I had any siblings, and I told them I didn't. I was being honest because I didn't know about Matt then.

"But I put two and two together and I realized that his DNA must have connected him to the crime, in their eyes. So I warned him. He had no idea what I was talking about; he barely even remembered the murders. But I convinced him to leave until we could figure out what to do.

"He left, and I heard nothing else until the news said he was arrested. He didn't do this, Mr. Carpenter. Like I said, he didn't even really remember the murders until I reminded him."

"And you believed him." It's a statement, not a question, and unnecessary, since she clearly believes him.

"He's family," she says, as if that explains everything, and it probably does.

"Where is your father now?"

"He passed away about a year ago. Believe it or not, the way I found out was by googling his name. He was living in New Hampshire; based on what I could tell, it was a heart attack."

"Could he have had other children besides the two of you?"

"I suppose so, but I'm not aware of any. Of course, I wasn't aware of Matt for all that time."

The truth is that it doesn't matter if Mary Pat and Matt had other siblings. It was Matt's DNA that was found on the scene. If he had an identical twin, then it could matter, but that seems like a long shot.

"So Matt asked you to convince me to stay and defend him?" I ask, confronting the elephant in the room.

She smiles. "No, I came up with that on my own. Look, I know he can't pay you, but my husband, Frank, and I, we have some money. I can give you seventy-five dollars a week for as long as it takes to pay the full amount, and I know that can be a very long time."

I hear a huge moan, and I realize that it is coming from me. It's not audible to anyone else, it's only in my head, but it's loud and anguished.

"This is not about money, Mary Pat."

"You're the only chance he has."

"Okay. I'll do it." I look around to see who said that, then realize it was me. I'm hoping I didn't say it out loud, but the look on her face says that I did.

After a beat she says, "You just surprised me."

"You and me both."

"I knew you would help. You wouldn't have come up here in the first place if you weren't a good person who believed in Matt."

I don't want to tell her that I don't particularly believe or disbelieve in Matt, that I don't even know Matt. There is a loud cheer in the bar, but it has nothing whatsoever to do with me agreeing to defend Matt Jantzen. J. D. Martinez has just hit a home run for the Red Sox, and I can see by the TV that they are up six–nothing.

Maybe I'll get comfortable up here; being surrounded by Yankee haters can't be all bad.

My guilt about abandoning Jantzen, which obviously no longer applies, is now replaced by my guilt at having agreed to take the case without consulting Laurie. She is going to bear the brunt of this.

When I get back to the hotel, I call her. "There has been a development," I say, which is obviously understating the case.

"I've got it all figured out" is her surprising response. "You'll come home, we'll get Ricky packed up, and we'll drop him off at camp together. Then I'll stay there with you for as long as the case takes and will help in the investigation. I've already spoken to Corey and Marcus, and they are prepared to come up if needed."

Corey Douglas and Marcus Clark are Laurie's partners in an investigation firm that they call the K Team, named in honor of Corey's ex-police-dog partner, a German shepherd named Simon Garfunkel. Simon is also an integral part of the team.

"So you already knew I was going to do this?"

"With one hundred percent certainty."

"How? Why?"

"Andy, you are the least self-aware person I know. So I have to fill that gap."

"My fee for doing this is zero, and there are going to be significant expenses."

"We have plenty of money," she says accurately.

"The case has been described to me as a stone-cold loser."

"We've heard that before."

"A defense attorney said it."

"I never trusted defense attorneys."

"We might be defending a double murderer."

"He saved a dog," she says. "Isn't that the bottom line?"

"Apparently it is."

need to adjust my theory of life.

I've always believed that humans function based on the enjoyment principle. That means that they ultimately do that which they enjoy, that which gives them pleasure.

Sometimes it's not a direct relationship between the action and the pleasure. For example, they might dislike their job, but enjoy what they can do with the money they make from doing it. My theory held that everything that we do is self-serving, even when we are being altruistic.

If we help others, it's because we enjoy doing so.

Don't ask me why.

But my new outlook flips the theory on its head, while still maintaining some of the basic premise. As powerful as our need for enjoyment is, the need to avoid pain and misery is even more consuming.

My current situation is a case in point, and I'll have time to focus on it on the drive back from Maine. I am going to dislike having a client and doing lawyer stuff; that's a given. It is hard, pressure-filled work and will not be remotely enjoyable. I'm more into easy, relaxed stuff.

But if I didn't do it, I'd feel an intense guilt that would be even worse than doing the work. And it wouldn't be time sensitive; it would stay with me. The case and trial, if there is one, will run its course and be over. The guilt would stay with me for as long as Matt Jantzen languished in prison, which would most likely be the rest of both of our lives.

Of course, in a perfect world, I would be able to avoid the work and also avoid the guilt. I am not nearly evolved enough for that yet, but it gives me something to aspire to. Compensating for regret and remorse is like karate: there are various levels of achievement and expertise.

Don't misunderstand; I'm good at it. Compared to the average person on the street, I'm a black belt in guilt avoidance. But there are higher levels to achieve; someday I am going to be a master.

So the bottom line is that taking on the case is opting for the lesser of the two miseries. It's a selfish act and I'm comfortable with that.

I actually enjoy it.

I stop at the jail to tell my new client that he is my new client.

"My sister convinced you?"

"She did. You have a persuasive sister."

"I told her not to speak to you, while secretly hoping she would. I never expected it would work."

"Nor did I. Now tell me where you were and what you were doing back at the time of the murders."

"Well, I certainly have no recollection of where I was that night. At that time I was working at Renys; it's a chain of department stores here in Maine. I was an assistant manager of the Damariscotta store."

I'm familiar with Renys; there is one next door to King Eider's that sells clothing, and another across the street that sells everything else that exists in the world, at ridiculously low prices.

"You grew up here?"

"Yes, in a town not far from here called Bremen. I lived here my whole life. It wasn't an easy decision to leave, but I needed to get away."

"How long after the murders did you leave town?"

"I'm not sure; maybe a few weeks? The murders were not really top of mind for me. They were just something I saw on the news. I remember it as a pretty big story here. I can figure out when I left, and then we can compare it to the date of the murders."

"Do that and let me know. Why did you leave Maine?"

"Things just weren't going well for me. I had just broken up with my girlfriend; or more accurately, she had broken up with me. My mother had died not that long before of Alzheimer's, and a friend had died of a blood disease. I was obviously very bummed about all of that. I had no family left here, at least none that I knew about, so it felt like a good time to go elsewhere and get a fresh start."

"Where did you go?"

He smiles. "I literally threw a dart at a map. It landed in Atlanta; I'm just glad my aim wasn't worse. I could have wound up in Beirut. I went to work at an office supply store . . . they made me an assistant manager.

"When I found out about my sister, I realized that Maine was home, especially since I now had family here. I figured I could get a job here easily enough, maybe eventually open my own store."

"How did you wind up in Paterson? Another dart?"

"No, that just happened. But I wasn't planning to stay there;

I was just trying to figure out how to deal with the accusations in Maine."

"Any possibility that you have an identical twin?"

He seems surprised by the question and smiles. "No chance; my mother was not the type to ever give up a child, no matter what. I guess she was the opposite of my father."

"Did you know your father well?"

He shakes his head. "Never met him. They were never married, and he apparently viewed my mother's pregnancy as a reason to bail out and not look back. I don't think they were together very long at all. My sister found out that he died last year."

"What made you send your DNA in to that service?"

"Funny thing is, it wasn't a big decision to me. I saw a commercial on television for it, and it got me to thinking that maybe my father had some other kids somewhere, or maybe I had some cousins I didn't know about. I never expected it to actually happen. When I sent it in, I wasn't even sure I'd contact any relatives I found.

"But then, when I heard about Mary Pat being back here in Maine . . . I don't know . . . I guess I just wanted to connect to family."

"And you have no idea whatsoever how your DNA wound up at the murder scene?"

"None at all. I was not there. I don't even know where the murder scene was."

I tell Matt to write down everything he can remember about that time, and that I will see him in about ten days. I head back to the hotel to check out.

On the way I call Charlie Tilton. "I need you to work on this case with me."

"Haven't we already had this conversation? Do you have some kind of need for ongoing rejection?"

"Girls in high school used to ask me the same question. But this is a different conversation, with a different request."

"Same client?" he asks, clearly suspicious.

"Same client."

"You said you need help. Does that mean you took the case? You're not bailing out?"

"Correct."

"Sucker."

"I won't argue with that characterization. But I need somebody local to teach me the lay of the land, and to do the backup work . . . filing briefs, dealing with the paperwork . . ."

"No trial work?"

"No. I'll handle that. You'll be the power behind the throne."

"Has your client suddenly come into a cash infusion?"

"Yeah, me. I'll pay your fee, which I hope and expect will be an amount reflecting the small-town environment we are in."

"Allow me to repeat myself: sucker."

"I've been called worse. What do you say? It's a chance for you to watch and learn from a legal genius."

"Meaning you?"

"Modesty forbids my saying so."

He pauses; I can almost hear him thinking through the phone. "Okay, I'm in."

"Sucker."

Damn, it is good to be home.

Being home never used to be important to me. I was always the focal point of my own existence, so wherever I was, I wasn't missing anything. My world went with me. If I was there, it was home.

Now, with Laurie and Ricky, it's different. Wherever they are is home, and that is where I want to be. It's a feeling I've had to get used to, because in a way it's disconcerting. For the first time, I'm emotionally dependent on others, which represents a loss of control. But the good outweighs the not so good.

By a lot.

Laurie is heavily into pre-camp mode, buying every piece of boy's camp clothing ever invented and sewing labels onto all of them. Since the kids are only allowed to take one trunk with them, Laurie will masterfully fill up every square inch of available space with stuff that Ricky will never wear. Basically he wears one T-shirt and one pair of underwear the entire summer.

I call upon my new legal partner, Charlie Tilton, to get the discovery documents and send them to me, making copies for himself and for our files.

"We don't have files," he says accurately.

"File creation is part of your job. Didn't I go over that in the interview?"

"No, but I'm on it, boss."

I should get the discovery within a couple of days and will go through it carefully. In the meantime I'll have time to reflect on why the hell I took on a client.

Usually when I start a case, I call a meeting of our whole team to bring them up-to-date and prepare them for what awaits us. There's no need to do that now since most of the gang will be staying here. At this point only Laurie will be with me up in Maine. If she needs additional investigative help, we'll either hire local or call and ask Marcus and Corey to come up, depending on what she needs.

I call Sam Willis, who holds the dual position of my accountant and our team's cyber-investigator. Sam can find out anything and everything online . . . he is a genius on the computer. Sometimes his work is even legal, though I am not one of those lawyers who is a stickler for the law.

I tell Sam about the case and give him his initial assignment. "Find out whatever you can about the murders, just from available media reports for now. But get the date that they were committed, and see if there's any way you can learn Matt Jantzen's whereabouts on that date.

"Check his credit card records; maybe he paid for a dinner fifty miles away at that very moment. Check his phone records; maybe you can place him making a call from the White House at the time of the killings. Matt doesn't know where he was, so let's see if we can learn it on our own. Anything you can find out, I can use."

"I'm on it." Sam would say "I'm on it" if I asked him to pick up my dry cleaning on Mars this afternoon. The good news is that he always is, in fact, "on it."

My next call is to Edna, who is always "off it." Edna is my office manager / admin, and her main goal is to do as little work as possible. Edna has almost no job responsibility other than to cash her checks, so she performs her job flawlessly.

"We have a client" is how I start the conversation, only so that I can hear the sound of her heart hitting the floor.

"Again?"

"It's been six months, Edna."

"Time flies."

I go on to tell her that the client is in Maine, so she will have almost nothing to do. There might be minimal clerical stuff, and she will deal with Charlie Tilton on sending materials to New Jersey while I'm here, but that is basically it.

"That sounds doable." Relief drips from her voice.

"If anybody can get it done, you can."

My last call is to Eddie Dowd. Eddie is a recent addition to our legal team; he's a great lawyer who is especially valuable to me because he doesn't mind doing boring lawyer stuff like preparing briefs.

As an ex-Giants football player, he tends to talk in sports clichés, of which there are millions.

I tell him about the case, and he's willing to go to Maine if needed.

"I'm in the bullpen warming up."

"I doubt it will be necessary, Eddie, but I appreciate the offer."

"Okay, you're the head coach." He tends to mix up his sports metaphors.

"Great. If I get in foul trouble, I'll call you."

I put Ricky to bed, a ritual that I've missed the last few days. We talk about the Mets; he's a bigger fan than I am and brings me up-to-date on what I've missed while away.

"You looking forward to camp?"

"Yeah. Is that okay? I mean, I'll miss you and Mom."

"It's very okay, Rick. We want you to have fun."

"Thanks, Dad. I love you."

Maybe I'll get tired of hearing that someday, but it won't be anytime soon.

Laurie is waiting for me in the den with a couple of glasses of wine. "We need to talk," she says.

"Uh-oh." Needing to talk, like needing to drink or needing to escape, is rarely a good thing. "What is it?"

"I think it's a major mistake for you to stay here for the ten days until we take Ricky to camp. You can go back, work on the case, and meet us at the camp the day I bring him there."

"That has a singular lack of appeal for me."

"Me too. But you know that every day in case preparation is precious, and to waste ten days here is crazy. I'll bring Tara, Sebastian, and Hunter with us when I take Ricky to camp."

"This is getting worse and worse. And it's your fault."

"My fault? How do you figure that?"

"If you had gotten to the dog-kicking guy first and kicked his ass, then Jantzen wouldn't have been arrested, and I wouldn't have a client."

"If I kicked his ass badly enough, maybe I would have been your client."

"Yeah, but you could afford my fee."

"You know I'm right about not waiting the ten days. That's why you're reacting like this."

"You know, you should be careful what you wish for. I'm a hotshot lawyer, so there are probably groupies waiting for me up there. And groupies travel in groups."

"That's okay. I'm willing to share you."

Tara is going to approve of her new surroundings.

I've taken the biggest suite they have here at the inn, and also an adjoining room. So all in all it's the equivalent of a pretty big apartment, with a bunch of sofas and chairs and beds for Tara and Hunter to comfortably lounge on. It's also carpeted, so Sebastian, who won't make the effort to get up on a couch or bed if they are six inches high, will be comfortable as well.

When Laurie gets here with the three of them, we're going to need the space. That is especially true since it will also function as my legal office for the duration. Charlie Tilton has also offered to share his office with me, but I doubt that I'll be taking him up on that very much.

I've told Charlie that I'm back in town, but I haven't contacted Matt Jantzen yet. My plan is to spend a lot of time in the room going through the discovery documents, trying to orient myself to the facts of the case.

As I go through it, the good news is that not a lot ties Matt to the crime. There is no conclusive evidence that he knew the victims, and if anything was taken in the apparent robbery, none of the stolen property was ever connected to him.

It's also a positive that Jantzen has no history of arrests or convictions. If he committed this horrible crime, in the eyes of the law it was a one-off. He has not been charged or even suspected of anything before or since; if he has, the police are unaware of it so far.

Interestingly, drugs were found in the toxicology conducted as part of the Charkin autopsy. He was taking opioids at a level that speaks to an addiction. It could be a positive for our defense, depending on where he was getting those drugs. Drugs and violence are all too compatible.

The only one piece of bad news is a beauty. Blood, at well more than just trace levels, was found on the right hand of one of the victims, Peter Charkin. The blood was on the knuckles and under two of the fingernails. The police theory of the case is that Charkin physically resisted and punched and scratched at his killer.

That blood DNA has been identified as Matt's. In the eyes of the police, and no doubt in the eyes of the jury, it is as damning as if Matt had taken a selfie video of himself committing the crime.

I can and will attack it on chain-of-custody grounds and faulty testing procedures, but those rarely succeed. At the end of the day the jury will believe that Matt Jantzen's blood was on the victim's hands.

I have no doubt that the police are continuing to investigate; it is fair to say that their work has just begun. Now that they have a name to attach to the DNA, there will be many more leads to follow. I expect more discovery to stream in and therefore possibly more shoes to drop.

For now, and I hope something will happen to change my view, there is little chance that we can prove Matt did not commit this crime. We have no alibi; even he has no idea where he was that night. So we are going to have to demonstrate either that someone else did it, or at least that someone else might have done it.

But no matter what we learn, or what we can show, we are going to have to somehow deal with Matt's blood being found on the hands of one of the victims. It's pretty hard to come up with an innocent explanation for that.

The police did plenty of investigating back around the time of the murders and came up with a couple of "persons of interest." This gives me areas to get into, though in each case the suspects were eliminated when their DNA did not match that which was on Charkin's hands.

Faced with a situation like this, I would ordinarily take Tara for a walk. She is going to love Maine. No more boring walks to Eastside Park in Paterson; this area of Maine is like a dog-walking Disneyland.

Today I scout out a future walk by going to Dodge Point. It's a scenic, easy walk, with no shrubbery and therefore no danger of winding up with ticks. And it's flat; no uphill climbs. Exactly the kind of walk that I like. Tara will eat it up; these are sights and especially smells that she will be unfamiliar with. Her tail will not stop wagging from the time we get out of the car to the time we are back at the inn.

I wish she were here.

Unfortunately, even though this promises to be a great vacation for Tara and her two friends, I am here to work. I've got to do some investigating to earn the money I'm paying myself to handle the case.

It starts tomorrow.

My father used to say, "You can't tell the players without a scorecard."

He certainly didn't make the phrase up, but he was using it to teach me a legal and investigative lesson. He was saying that you need to have a game plan, a script to follow, that identifies everyone and their agendas. Only then could you weed out what was important from the clutter and noise.

My client has little to offer in this regard because his claim, his defense, is that he had nothing to do with the murders or the victims. It's a consistent and logical position to take; how can he provide insight into something he knows nothing about?

To make matters worse, he is not even pretending to have an alibi. He has no more recollection of where he was on a particular night two years ago than I do, though in my case there's a pretty good chance I was at Charlie's Sports Bar.

My scorecard, such as it is, will have to be the police investigation. The murder book will tell me all the work they did before they came to believe, two years after the fact, that Matt Jantzen was the guilty party. They conducted a bunch of interviews and even identified possible suspects.

I will retrace their steps. A lot of it will be to no avail; witnesses are unlikely to tell me anything different from what they told the police. To complicate matters further, memories fade and become much less precise over time.

But maybe those conversations will lead me in other directions that might be productive. I won't know until I know, but hovering over everything will be Matt's blood on the victim's hand.

My first stop is a small café attached to the bookstore in a building that houses the Lincoln Theater upstairs. Just down the block is the Skidompha Library; we are clearly in the cultural center of Damariscotta.

I'm meeting with Carole Peterson, who is Matt Jantzen's ex-girlfriend. He had told me that their breakup was one of the reasons he left Maine in the first place.

I had reached Carole by phone, and she suggested the café as a meeting place. She said that she worked nearby, though didn't say where, and offered to talk to me during her coffee break. This is definitely a good place to have a coffee break; their scones look fantastic.

"So you're trying to help Matthew?" she asks, once we're settled. It's the first time I've heard him referred to in any way other than Matt.

"I am. I'm hoping you can help me do that."

"How?"

"Just by telling me about him. About your recollections."

"I don't know how much there is to tell. We went out for a couple of years; we even talked about getting engaged. But we were young, and things changed."

She talks about having been young as though it were decades ago. People don't generally age that much in two years.

"I should say that Matt changed."

"How so?"

"He got moody, very critical of everything, especially things

I did. Looking back, I should have realized that he had a lot going on. Maybe I would have . . . could have . . . been more understanding. But at the time it just made me want out."

"What was going on?"

"Well, for one thing, his mother had died a few months before. Then he lost his friend . . . our friend . . . Carl Blanchard . . . to cancer. Some kind of leukemia, I think. That was hard on him. But he also wasn't getting anywhere career-wise. His job was okay, but he wanted to be his own boss."

"So you ended it?"

She nods. "I did. I'm sure that just added to his depression, or whatever it was. We dropped out of touch, but I heard that he left town about a month or so after that. I can't be sure of the timing."

"When did the murders take place, as it relates to your breaking up and him leaving?"

"I think it was about two weeks after the breakup. I remember because I was so upset at hearing the news, and I had no one to reach out to. Matt could have been that person, but it was too late for that."

"Why were you so upset about the murders?"

"Tina Welker was my friend. I used to work part-time at Augusta General, where she was a nurse. I worked in reception. We were pretty close; she was an easy person to talk to."

This is jolting news, and not in a positive way. "Did Matt know her?"

Carole pauses. "I've been thinking about that. I don't know if he ever met her; they were in different parts of my life. He probably did, but I can't be sure."

"Why do you say he probably did?"

"Because this is a small-town area. A lot of us went to the same high school, but there aren't that many places for young people to hang out, you know? It would be weird if he never ran into her, but whether they were friends or not, I don't remember that they were."

"Would she have known you and Matt were going out?"

"Oh, definitely. I used to talk to Tina about Matt and our situation, and she was one of the people who advised me to end it. My friends were pretty much all saying that."

Uh-oh. "Did you ever tell Matt what Tina said?"

She shrugs. "Probably. He certainly knew what my friends thought about it. I honestly don't know if I mentioned Tina specifically."

"You said 'probably.'"

Another shrug. "I guess I should have said 'maybe.' I really don't remember." Then, "Why would they have arrested Matt? What makes them think he did such a terrible thing?"

I answer that with another question. "What do you think? Would he be capable of doing something like that?"

She shakes her head. "No way," she says with conviction. "Absolutely not."

"Why do you say that?"

"The Matt I knew is a good person. He had a temper, but if he was mad at you, you probably deserved it. And if you did something wrong, he would let you know it."

"So don't kick a dog in front of him?"

She smiles. "You definitely don't want to do that. He loves dogs."

We live in an interconnected world, but cops take it to a new level.

Cops just know other cops, whether they work with them or not. And the cops they know always know other cops, and so on and so on. So if one cop wants to get in touch with another one, anywhere, he can do so with little effort.

Kevin Bacon needs six degrees; Sergeant Anyone can do it in three.

The same thing holds true for ex-cops; apparently club membership is permanent. Fortunately I have strong connections to two ex-cops. There's Laurie, who I happen to be married to, and Corey Douglas, her partner in the K Team.

Between them they have arranged an appointment for me in Portland to talk to Captain Dustin Oliver of the Maine State Police, Robbery-Homicide Division. Oliver was in charge of the investigation that has ultimately resulted in Matt's arrest.

I'm surprised that Captain Oliver agreed to talk with me so easily. In a similar situation, police officers in New Jersey would have avoided this meeting like the plague. Of course, police officers in New Jersey know me, while Oliver doesn't. That would explain a lot.

"Lieutenant Collier said to say hello" is how I start, as I was instructed to do. Collier is a cop that Corey Douglas knew, and Collier in turn knows Captain Oliver.

He smiles. "How is Lieutenant Collier?"

I have no idea how he is; I've never laid eyes on him. So I say, "Fine. He's the same as ever."

"Is he? Then he must have changed some, because Lieutenant Collier is a woman."

"Maybe she was undercover. But I did notice she was clean-shaven." Then, "The truth is I never met or spoke to Lieutenant Collier, but I know people who must know her, because here I am."

"No problem," he says agreeably.

"I'm a defense attorney," I say, getting all the bad news out at once.

"I'm not a huge fan of defense attorneys." Then, "Come on, you think I would not have checked you out before agreeing to this meeting?"

"I assumed you had."

"So with the understanding that I won't discuss details about the investigation, ask your questions."

"When was the first time you heard the name Matt Jantzen?"

"About three weeks ago, when we hit the DNA match through that website."

"You have someone checking those sites?"

Oliver nods. "Yup. Second time we got a hit. Those things are fantastic; it's like a confession hotline."

"But he never came up in your investigation before that?"

"You got the discovery, right? Then you know he didn't. He committed the perfect crime, until he didn't."

"What can you tell me about Sergeant Rojas?" Sergeant Anthony Rojas is the forensics officer who handled the case, which means he retrieved the blood from the victim's hand that was determined to be Matt's. Forensics will be everything in this trial.

"Tony? Good man. The best."

"Can you get me in to talk to him?"

Oliver frowns. "That's way above my pay grade. Tony died about six months ago. Heart attack."

This is not good news, and I don't just mean for Sergeant Rojas and his family. I'm likely going to have to attack the collection and chain of custody of the DNA evidence, and dead people are by far the most difficult to trap and embarrass on the witness stand.

"You've had some chain-of-custody issues up here." I don't know of any, so at this point I'm fishing. Maybe he'll inadvertently point me in a right direction.

He seems amused. "Really? I'm not aware of any. But you should talk to Steinkamp about that, not that he'll help you much. If I know George, he's chomping at the bit to go head-to-head with you."

Oliver's talking about the prosecuting attorney, who I saw at the arraignment but haven't spoken to yet. "Why is that?"

"Come on, you're a famous New York lawyer."

"New Jersey."

"Whatever."

I have some difficult questions for Captain Oliver, but since he is very much alive, I'm going to save them for when he is under oath in front of a jury.

"Let me ask you something," I say. "Something that isn't in the discovery. You stopped working on the case because you had nowhere to go with it, and—"

"I never stop working on cases. I put some to the side and come back to them. This one I came back to often; get my wife on the stand and ask her how many nights I've gone over that murder book. For some reason she doesn't find it terribly romantic."

I nod. "Fair enough. When you originally put it aside, that was obviously because you couldn't get enough evidence to make an arrest. But at the time, who was at the top of the suspect list? Who did you think, down deep, was the most likely person to have done this?"

He thinks about this for a few moments. "I can't give you a name because it's a person I could never identify. I have my suspicions, but it's the one piece of information I wanted to know but could never get."

"You had a suspect in mind? Who?"

He shakes his head. "I'm not going there; I don't name people unless I can back it up. But the truth is that Charkin was taking opioids; it's highly likely that he was addicted or becoming addicted. All I can say is that I was never able to find out where he was getting the drugs. I never found his dealer."

"Are opioids a big problem up here?" For some reason I don't think of places like this having the same issues as big cities, but I'm sure they must have their share.

He nods. "Borderline out of control. Bigger than it was even two years ago, that's for sure."

"So you know more about the dealers now?"

"Definitely. I've personally put a few away, but there's always someone to take their place. Drug-dealing teams have deep benches."

"That's because it pays well."

"Yeah. But it's just as well that I never found Charkin's dealer."

"Why?"

"Because if I had, he would have been suspect number one. But he would have been the wrong guy. Matt Jantzen is the right guy."

Tina Welker is Carole's friend Tina?"

I've just told my client that Tina Welker, one of the murder victims, was the friend of Carole Peterson, his ex-girlfriend.

It's the second time that I've seen Matt since I came back up here to Maine. I've only been here five days, but if feels like a month. Time moves slowly when no progress is being made.

"That's the very one. Did you ever meet her?"

He thinks for a while before answering. "I can't say for sure, but probably. Carole sometimes took me to parties her friends had, so if Tina was at any of them, then there's a pretty good chance we met. But nothing stands out."

"Did Carole ever tell you that Tina advised her to break things off with you?"

"No. That I would have remembered. Did Carole say that?"

"She thought so but wasn't sure. By the time Steinkamp is finished with her, she'll quote the conversation you had word for word."

"He'll get her to lie?"

"Think of it as memory enhancement."

"So the theory is that I found out that Tina didn't think Carole should stay with me, and I responded by shooting her and another guy in the head?"

"Basically, yes."

"And there are people on the planet that will believe that?" Matt appears incredulous at the prospect.

"It fits the narrative. Juries will be inclined to believe you did it because of the blood on the scene. This just gives them a confirming reason, although they don't need one. The state does not have to demonstrate or prove motive."

"My blood could not have been on the scene. I know I keep saying that, and I'm sorry, but it's the truth."

"In the eyes of the world, and that world includes the future members of the jury, the blood was there. We will try to attack it based on various technical factors, but we won't succeed."

"So we've lost already?" He's obviously and understandably frustrated.

I nod. "That battle is as good as lost. We will fight the good fight, but that ship has sailed. So we will come at this from another angle, which happens to be the only angle available to us."

"What's that?"

"We will try to prove that someone else did it, and we will have to name that someone. If we do, then it won't matter how your blood got there. Bleeding in a specific place is not a crime; if someone else is the killer, then you are not."

"So you're going to solve a crime that the police couldn't for two years?"

"I said we would try. I didn't say anything about succeeding."

"That's not really what I want to hear."

"I know that. But if it's any consolation, we have one advantage that the police did not have. Besides our brilliance."

"What's that?"

"They had the blood DNA. They were positive that it was left by the killer, so any suspects that they had were automatically eliminated by their DNA not matching. We come at it with the assumption that the blood is either not yours, or planted, or whatever. So potential suspects that were eliminated in their eyes are not eliminated in ours."

"You keep saying 'we' and 'our.' Are you talking about you and me or are there some other people on our team?"

"My wife, Laurie, is a trained investigator, and she will be here in a few days. And we may bring up at least one other member of their investigative team."

"This has to be costing money."

I smile. "We're in it for the glory. Did you prepare the list?"

"Yes." He takes a piece of paper from his pocket and hands it to me. It's a list of friends and associates he had back around the time he left Maine the first time, shortly after the murders. It gives us people to talk to; maybe one of them will remember that the night of the murder they were with Matt in Vegas, or Paris, or anywhere other than at the murder scene.

"This is everyone I can think of. Not all of them will remember me."

I look at the list briefly before refolding it and putting it in my own pocket. "Okay, if you think of anything that might be helpful, you know how to reach me. If I'm not at the hotel, I'll be sucking down lobster rolls somewhere."

"They're pretty good, huh? That's one thing I missed when I moved to Atlanta."

"Outstanding. I would stop and have one now, but I'm already going to be late for a meeting."

"About the case?"

"Yeah. I'm going to see the guy who wants to put you in prison for the rest of your life. I'll give him your regards."

When I enter George Steinkamp's office, a dog greets me at the door.

He's some kind of grayish poodle mix, no more than a dozen pounds. He's adorable and his tail is wagging, a sure sign that he doesn't know I am a defense attorney.

"Toby Allen, show some manners." George Steinkamp smiles. "No sniffing people you haven't been introduced to."

"I'm Andy," I say to Toby Allen. Then, to Steinkamp, "Your dog has a different last name? Maybe from a previous marriage?"

He laughs. "It's a middle name. We have a neighbor with a dog named Toby, so this distinguishes him."

"This is a dog-friendly area. Everybody seems to have one."

Steinkamp nods. "A friend once observed that in California everyone wants to know what kind of car you drive. In the South it's which church you attend. And here it's what kind of dog you have."

"I've got a couple myself."

He nods. "I know. You've got a whole rescue foundation as well."

"You've been checking me out."

Another nod. "Advance scouting. Always good to know the opposition."

"It doesn't have to be that way. You can drop the case and we can go picnicking with our dogs."

He smiles. "I think not. But as much as I'm enjoying our chat, sit down and let's talk about the case. I expect it won't take long."

I sit in the chair across from his desk, and he and Toby Allen retreat behind it. "We here in Maine, and I assume it's true in New Jersey as well, prefer to avoid trials. They're expensive and usually we know how they will turn out anyway."

"So you here in Maine, like New Jersey, offer plea arrangements?"

"We do. Sometimes I'm in favor of them, and sometimes I'm not. But often, as in this case, it's not my decision."

I can turn him down now or wait for the offer. I decide to wait, just to see what it reveals about how he views the strength of the state's case.

"So . . . forty to life, no possibility of parole."

"Dogs are great, aren't they?" I ask. "Although I'm not crazy about the face licking. I'm not sure why they do that."

"He killed two people. Put a gun to their heads and blew their brains out."

"The jury returned a verdict already? The least they could have done is call me and let me know. I didn't even get a chance to thank them for their service."

"Jantzen left a signed confession at the scene. Actually, better than that, because confessions can be forged."

"He pled not guilty because he's not guilty."

"So you're turning this down? Want to talk to your client first?"

"Yes, as to the turning it down. No, as to talking to my client."

"Fair enough. I'm glad you feel that way. When crimes like

this are committed, I prefer it when a jury has a chance to weigh in."

"I'm happy for you."

He smiles. "You liking it here? We've got everything you have in the big city . . . moving-picture shows, restaurants where you sit down and get cloth napkins . . . bakeries with fancy bread-slicing machines . . . you name it."

"If it's so great, how come I can't get a decent lobster roll?"

He smiles, knowing that I'm joking. "Yeah, that's a big problem around here."

I turn to Toby Allen. "I've some family coming up that you would love. Let's arrange a playdate."

It's getting close to dinnertime; the older I get the more comfortable I am with eating early. Before I know it I'll be sucking down oatmeal through a straw for lunch and going out for the early-bird dinner.

So I head for King Eider's. I'm finding that I like the nightly ritual of eating at the bar with my new buddies, none of whose names I know. I'm even sort of getting into the Red Sox, and not just when they play the Yankees.

At around ten o'clock I leave with the game in the seventh inning. I want to get back in time to call Laurie before she goes to sleep. I walk to my car, which is not in the main parking lot, because that lot was full when I arrived.

When I get back there, I'm almost at my car when I hear a voice say, "Hold it right there, lawyer."

I don't like the sound of this at all, and not just because I hate being identified as a lawyer. I turn, and two guys are standing in front of a pickup truck with those huge wheels that make the truck seem fifteen feet all. They are big guys, well suited to driving this truck.

"Hiya, fellas." It's as clever a line as I can come up with under the circumstances.

"We don't like you helping that killer, and we're going to show you how much we don't like it."

"Okay, I hear you. Let me just deal with one thing first, and then we can talk it out."

"We're not here to talk."

"I understand. Just give me a second."

I take out my phone and dial 911; it's not easy to do with my hands shaking. After a few seconds I talk into the phone. "Two guys are threatening me in the parking lot on Elm Street, across from the used-book store. License plate ERW548. Thank you."

I disconnect the phone and turn to the two guys. "Okay, we have just a couple of minutes before the cops come. Although you probably shouldn't do anything stupid, since they have your license plate number."

They turn and start climbing into their truck, but the guy getting into the driver's seat takes the time to say, "You just made a big mistake, lawyer."

They leave, and once I'm sure they're gone, I do as well. There's no sense waiting for the police, since I don't get cell service back here and never reached 911.

Now my only question is whether to tell Laurie about this incident when I call her. The negative is that it will cause her to worry, and the positive is that I will appear heroic.

I'm definitely going to tell her.

think Marcus should come up there," Laurie says. "At least until I can get there . . . maybe he should stay a few days longer than that."

Perhaps I shouldn't have told Laurie about the evening's events. Rather than praising my heroism, she's telling me that I need protection.

"I can handle these guys myself." We both know this claim is patently ridiculous.

"Andy, don't take this the wrong way, but you said they left in their truck."

"So?"

"So if they're old enough to drive, you can't handle them yourself. You might be able to outsmart them, like you obviously did tonight, but you can't count on doing that every time."

"It's fine. I'll be careful."

"Marcus can pay them a quick visit; he can reason with them."

Marcus Clark is one of the three human members of the K Team, Laurie's investigative group. I would say that he is also the toughest, scariest human being on earth, but that might be too limiting. Five minutes with Marcus and the two big guys from the parking lot would be begging me to go fishing with them.

The truth is that it would be a relief to have Marcus up here looking out for me, but there's no way I will ever admit that. I'm not sure why that is. I'm a physical coward and Laurie knows that to be true no matter what I say. Yet I try to maintain what we both know is a ridiculous façade.

"Laurie, I'm fine. If that changes, I'll let you know. I was hoping we could focus on my coolness in the face of danger. It was really something to behold."

"I choose to focus on the danger part." Then, apparently giving in, she asks, "How's the case going?"

"It isn't. I'm getting nowhere, which is no surprise, since I don't even know what I'm looking for."

"What do you mean?"

"Well, I have to operate under the assumption that Matt is innocent, otherwise I'm just spinning my wheels. That leaves three possibilities, and none of them stand out at this point."

"What are they?"

"One is that Peter Charkin was the target. Two is that Tina Welker was the target. The third possibility, the scariest one of all, is that it was just a robbery gone bad, a home invasion."

"Which makes it random."

"Right. And therefore almost impossible to solve. I can take apart the victims' lives, but if the victims had nothing to do with their killer, then it won't get me anywhere."

"So we focus on the two victims and hope it wasn't random."

"That's the plan," I say, with no enthusiasm whatsoever.

"We'll get there."

"Right. And it's not like I'm not making progress. I've only been here a week and I've already managed to piss off two big guys with a truck."

"By the way, there's a new plan for getting Ricky to camp."

"What do you mean?"

"He doesn't want me to take him. He wants to go on the camp bus with all the rest of the kids."

"Why?"

"Because he's growing up and he's at the age where being with his parents can be embarrassing."

"How long will that last?"

"Hard to say. At least a decade. Maybe until he has kids that are embarrassed by him."

"So that means I can't meet him at the camp when the bus arrives."

"You're catching on quickly. I know you're disappointed, Andy. So am I. But I'll drop him off at the bus and then head up to Maine. Tara, Sebastian, and Hunter will enjoy the ride."

"Any word from Hunter's previous owner?"

"Not so far."

"Maybe he's the guy you should send Marcus to visit."

I get off the phone so that I will have time to feel sorry for myself before I go to sleep. I'm missing everyone at home, which is probably why they call it home.

I think my outlook would be better if I were accomplishing something here, so I need to make that happen. To that end I pick up the discovery documents and read through them for the third time.

I'm going to show them how a hotshot, big-time New York lawyer from New Jersey operates.

My first stop is the Lincoln County Sheriff's Office.

Even though Damariscotta has its own small police department, it overlaps with the county sheriff's. Since the sheriff covers the whole area, this seems like the logical place to give my report.

I stop and speak to the officer manning the reception desk. The name tag on his chest says that he is Sergeant Melvin. I'm assuming that Melvin is a last name, so I don't introduce myself as Lawyer Andy.

"My name is Andy Carpenter. I want to report an incident that happened last night in Damariscotta. Two very large guys threatened me."

"Threatened you how?"

"I'm a defense attorney and they told me they would teach me a lesson because I'm representing a particular client."

"Wait a minute. Carpenter . . . are you the lawyer that's defending the guy who killed those two people?"

"Is *allegedly* a word that people ever use here in Maine?"

"Yeah, there are people that use it. Me . . . not so much."

"Anyway, here's the license number of their truck." I hand him a piece of paper on which I wrote the number.

He looks at it. "Did they do anything to you other than talk?"

"No."

He smiles. "You fought them off?"

"I outsmarted them."

"What do you expect us to do with this? Talking nasty isn't considered a capital crime around here."

"In a perfect world, you would give them a warning. At the very least, you'll have this in case something happens."

"I'll tell the sergeant."

"I imagine he'll call in a SWAT team?"

Another smile from Sergeant Melvin. "Something like that."

On the way to meet with Rachel Manning, I call Sam Willis. He answers on the first ring, as always. "Andy, talk to me."

"I need you to run down a license plate." I give him the number. "It's a Maine plate."

"You got it. I'll get back to you."

"Thanks. And just me, Laurie doesn't need to know about it."

"Roger."

"Roger doesn't need to know either."

Buoyed by somebody's having finally paid attention to me, I head up to Rockland, about a half hour north, to see Rachel Manning. Rockland is a town filled with restaurants, and Rachel works as a waitress at a place called Archer's.

It's right on the water, open and airy with glass walls providing a great view from every table. Lobster boats are visible out on the water; I hope they are productive, because I still have a lot of eating to do in my time here.

Because it's three thirty in the afternoon, no customers are eating here. As I walk in, a woman dressed in white waitress garb signals me from a table in the back. She's obviously been waiting for me and either recognizes me because I'm famous, or because I'm the only person likely to show up at this hour. I'm going to go with the famous explanation.

"Hi," she says. "Sorry to drag you all the way up here."

"No problem. Thanks for talking with me. Nice place."

She nods. "And we have the best lobster rolls in the state."

"I'll be the judge of that."

"Not until five o'clock; that's when the kitchen opens again."

We talk briefly about nothing in particular. She tells me that she has lived in Maine since she was one year old, but will never be considered a Mainer. "You've got to be born here. No exceptions. . . . But you wanted to talk about Tina Welker?"

"Yes. You were her friend?"

"Her best friend. We finished each other's sentences."

"That could get annoying," I say, for no other reason than I find it annoying when people do that to me.

She doesn't take offense. "It never did. I miss Tina every day. She really cared about people, which is probably why she had the job she had."

"She was a nurse," I say, though obviously Rachel would know that.

"Not just a nurse; she did radiation therapy on cancer patients. You don't do that unless you love people and want to do whatever you can."

"Did she talk to you about her boyfriends?"

"Of course. Every one of them."

"She dated a lot?"

Rachel nods. "Guys loved Tina. And Tina loved guys."

"Any of them jealous? Did she ever talk about one of them getting angry that she wasn't with them exclusively?"

Rachel shakes her head. "Not that I know of, and I would know. Tina always made it clear to her dates that she wasn't the 'going steady' type. She didn't sneak around behind anybody's back."

"Did she ever express concern for her safety? Ever mention anyone she might be afraid of?"

"No, not really afraid . . ."

"Somebody you think I should know about?"

"Well, there is that neighbor. I don't think he was a threat or anything; Tina didn't think so. But he gave me the creeps. I saw him a few weeks ago; that's why I'm thinking about it now."

"Which neighbor is that?"

"He lived a couple of houses down from her. He used to complain that she was making too much noise, playing music and that kind of stuff. But the people in the house between them never said anything."

I'm surprised that I haven't read anything about this in the discovery documents. "Did you ever tell this to the police?"

She shakes her head. "No, I don't think so."

"What is his name?"

"Not sure. Bennett, or Barnett, or something like that."

"Why was she concerned about him?"

Rachel shrugs. "I think he just bugged her; and she thought he stared at her a lot when she was outside. One time he sort of asked her out, said they should have coffee or something, but she wasn't interested. Anyway, thinking back, Tina was more concerned about the hang-ups."

The "hang-ups" Rachel is talking about were in the police reports. In the couple of weeks before the murder, Tina had complained to the phone company that she was getting crank calls from someone who would hang up when she answered the phone.

The cops were never able to determine who was making the calls; but they had a theory that it might have been the eventual killer trying to determine when she was home.

"Did she have any idea who was making those calls?" I say.

"Not that she ever told me."

"Did you know Peter Charkin?"

She frowns. "Yeah, I knew him."

"You didn't like him?"

"No, especially not for Tina. I think he was into drugs, and he always seemed to have money to throw around. He was just . . . I guess the word is *erratic*. But Tina liked him, so I never said anything. By the end, she was going out with only him, which was very unlike her. And . . ."

Rachel doesn't continue, just stops for a good ten seconds, so I say, "Usually the word *and* is followed by other words."

She nods. "And it didn't seem like he made her happy. I talked to her briefly on the phone the night before she . . . she died . . . and she was upset and really short with me. It wasn't like her."

"But she didn't say why?"

"No, but he was at her house, so I'm guessing they were having an argument or something."

"Did Tina ever do drugs?"

"Never. No chance. She didn't need them. Tina created her own happy, you know?"

The truck is owned by Henry Stokan. He's got something of a record: arrested twice for assault and once for possession with intent to sell drugs. One of the assault charges was dropped, and he got probation on the other. Got a year in jail for the drug charge; it was pled down to possession. He served six months."

To get all this, Sam must have broken into either police or court records, though it's possible it was available in public documents. I'm not inclined to ask how he got it, just in case it's illegal. I'm okay either way, but I prefer ignorance as a fallback position.

"Anything else on him?" I ask, but I've already heard enough to be stunned. Stokan was one of the tentative suspects in the original investigation, as documented in the discovery. Like everyone else, he was eliminated when his DNA did not match.

"Works construction for a company based in Augusta. Not married. I have other stuff . . . addresses at work and home . . . I can email you all of it."

"Thanks, Sam. Please do that."

I hang up and ponder the latest depressing development. The guy who threatened to assault me is a professional assaulter. I'm going to guess that the guy with him was not a mediator.

The only thing I can think of that might prevent them from trying again is that they think I gave the police their license plate when I fake-called 911.

Of course, I've really given it to the police since then, though I tend to doubt that the cop did anything with it. Either way, their having it doesn't protect me from assault, it merely points out the potential assaulters after the fact. I am much more interested in preventing the fact.

The interesting part of Sam's report is that Stokan was possibly involved in selling drugs. The toxicology report indicated that Charkin had opioids in his system, at a high level. Maybe Stokan doesn't want me to be investigating the murder not on behalf of society, but because he committed it.

It's unlikely, but it puts Stokan at the top of my list of suspects. Unfortunately, he's also at the bottom, since his is currently the only name on the list.

I stop off at Charlie Tilton's office to see how my top assistant is doing. He's just pulling up as I get here. "Sorry if you were waiting," he says, even though I hadn't mentioned that I was coming. "But work got in the way."

"You were in court?"

"No, I got a haircut. Looks good, huh? Fifteen bucks, but worth every penny."

"Getting a haircut is work?"

"Of course. What if I have to go to court? You want me to look unkempt?"

"Never. I think all lawyers should be totally kempt."

"Good. I'm trying to live up to your standards. And now I can expense the fifteen bucks."

We go up to his office and he makes us both coffee. For me coffee is like beer; I drink it because it's there and I feel like I'm supposed to, but I don't particularly like the taste.

Once we're settled, I ask, "Where does one go to buy drugs around here?"

"This case is really getting to you, huh?"

"Something like that. Charkin had opioids in his system. Where is he likely to have gotten them? I spoke to the cops and they said it's an answer they never came up with."

"Who did you speak to?"

"Captain Oliver. State police. It was his case."

"Good man, but he wasn't being straight with you. He knows where Charkin got the drugs, at least indirectly. What he meant was that he couldn't prove it."

I'm not surprised that Captain Oliver wasn't totally forthcoming, and I'm pleased that Charlie seems to have the information. "So what's the answer?"

"Jerry Donnelly. Known as Big Jerry, mostly because he's big and his name is Jerry."

"And he deals?"

Charlie nods. "Among other things. He's what would pass for organized crime in this area."

"Maine never struck me as an organized crime type of place."

"There's not going to be a war between the Five Families, and no one is going to the mattresses, but we have our share. And it all revolves around Jerry Donnelly. He commits crime and he's organized, so that would fit the textbook definition."

"So he would be capable of murder?"

"Oh, yes. No question about it."

"And where does he get the drugs to dispense?"

"That's a question that I don't think has ever been answered, or at least I'm not aware if it has. But drugs are the key to his operation; they bring in the most money, and the word is that Donnelly is hurting for money these days."

"Why?"

Charlie shrugs. "Organized crime doesn't pay like it used to, and there is a large employee payroll. Good people, or in this case bad people, don't come cheap."

"What about Henry Stokan?"

Tilton reacts in surprise. "Boy, you do get around. No legal grass grows under your feet. What is your connection to Stokan?"

"He doesn't want me representing Matt Jantzen; instead of filing a legal brief with the court, he threatened me in a parking lot."

"How did you get out of that one?"

"I told him you were Jantzen's lawyer."

"I hope that's big-city humor. Stay clear of Stokan; he's meaner than he is dumb, and he's really dumb. And as you already know, he's large."

"He had a friend with him the same size. I'm actually not sure which one was Stokan, although the one talking was the driver, and the truck is registered to Stokan. I'm getting a photo of him."

"Just be careful."

"Would he be connected to Donnelly?"

Tilton thinks for a moment. "Could be. Make that probably. Donnelly doesn't do his own dirty work."

S am says the guy who threatened you is dangerous," Laurie says.

"That's disappointing; I told Sam to keep it to himself. Sam obviously is not familiar with the concept of lawyer / computer-guy confidentiality."

"I forced it out of him. I told him I'd never make him another pancake if he didn't tell me everything."

"Everybody's got their price. But what he said was correct; even more than he knows." I tell her what Charlie Tilton told me about Stokan and Jerry Donnelly.

"You think either or both of them could be involved in the killings?"

"Right now your guess is as good as mine. Stokan could have just been pushing around the big-city lawyer and letting him know that he thinks Matt is a killer that shouldn't be defended. Or he could have been involved and doesn't want an investigation to uncover inconvenient facts."

"And Donnelly?"

"According to Charlie, if Charkin was taking drugs, then it's a good bet they somehow came through Donnelly. But I have no idea why Donnelly would have been inclined to kill a customer."

"Or set Matt up to take the fall. Have you asked Matt if he has any connection to Donnelly or Stokan?"

"No, but I will."

"And of course none of this explains the DNA."

Laurie has just put her finger on the main fact hovering over this case . . . the herd of elephants in the room. No matter what we uncover, we're eventually going to have to explain away the DNA.

Even proving that someone like Stokan was the killer wouldn't be enough. There would be nothing that would prevent Matt from being seen as his accomplice, present at the scene and attacked by Charkin, resulting in Matt's blood on his hand.

"You want to get to the unpleasant part of this conversation now?" she asks.

"You mean so far we've been having the fun part?"

"Marcus is coming up there tomorrow."

"We've been through this; I don't need him. I'm being careful and Stokan thinks I gave his license plate number to nine-one-one."

"Here's the mistake you're making. You're viewing this as a negotiation, as if we're trying to reach a decision that hasn't already been made. Marcus is coming up there tomorrow; he already knows about it. You can either reserve him a room or hopefully yours has a king bed."

Laurie clearly thinks she can intimidate me. Unfortunately, in this case I can't pretend to call 911, so I'm pretty much left without options. Marcus is coming, whether I like it or not, and the part of me that isn't an egotistical idiot likes it.

Marcus can handle Stokan and his friend without calling 911. Marcus could handle Russia without calling 911.

"Okay. Call me tomorrow and let me know what time Marcus will be here, and I'll meet him."

"Thank you," she says, as if I am doing her a favor.

"Does Marcus like lobster?"

"Have you ever come across something that Marcus doesn't eat?"

"No, but at some point we should do a tofu test."

I head down to the jail to talk to my client. I could have called him, but over the years I have learned that being locked up before trial tends to make people feel insecure. They fear that they have been forgotten and appreciate it when people pay attention to them. People such as their lawyers.

Like all such meetings, this one starts with the client asking about progress in the case. Matt wants me to say that I have achieved a breakthrough, and the charges are about to be dropped with an apology from the state.

Once I gently dispense with that fantasy, I ask, "Does the name Henry Stokan mean anything to you?"

"No."

I show him a photograph of Stokan that Sam has somehow gotten and emailed to me. It's a mug shot. "Do you recognize him?"

"No. Is that Stokan?"

"Yes. What about Jerry Donnelly? That name ring a bell?"

"It feels like it might, but I can't place it. Who are these people?"

"Bad guys. Stokan threatened me the other night, and Donnelly is said to run various criminal enterprises in this area."

"Why did Stokan threaten you?"

"For defending you."

"Is this guy involved in our case, or does he just dislike me?"

"I hope he's involved."

"Maybe he's the killer?" Matt asks.

"Hard to say, but he and Donnelly have potential. But having a motive or connection to the victims would help."

"I didn't have a motive or connection, but they think I did it."

"Your blood DNA was on the scene. If you're ever playing a game of 'motive, connection, DNA,' DNA beats everything."

When I get back to the hotel, Henry Stokan is waiting for me.

At least I think it's him. The truck looks the same, although I'm not exactly a truck aficionado. I know they're bigger than cars, but that's basically it.

Two people are in the truck. I can't make them out in the shadows, especially because I am almost directly behind them, but they look like large men. I'm going to assume one of them is Stokan; if I'm wrong, no harm, no foul. If I'm right, then also no harm, because I am not going anywhere near them.

The truck is running; the headlights are on. Maybe that's so they can have the air conditioner working. I can't be sure, and it's not particularly hot out. But if Stokan is trying to lie secretly in wait, he's not good at it. Either that or he is underestimating me and not expecting that I'll be watching out for him.

They haven't seen me, so it's pretty easy to avoid them. I just drive around to the back, make sure no other occupied cars are back there waiting for me, and park the car. I'm a little nervous about it because this area is darker and less likely to be observed by anyone, so I hurry from the car to the lobby door.

Once I make it inside, I head up the back stairs to my second-floor room, without going to the main lobby. When I'm safely in the room, I do a quick look around to make sure no unwanted visitors are inside, though I have no idea what I would do if I found one.

I can see the main parking lot from my window, so I look outside and confirm that the truck is still there. I'm not sure what I should do; I can't call the cops and expect them to come out because of a suspicious truck. I certainly have no proof that the two are waiting for me, or threatening me.

I don't even know if I want them to know I've evaded them or not. It could get them to leave, or possibly to try to get into my room.

I turn on the television and watch the Red Sox game. Every five minutes or so I peek out the window. Stokan, or whoever it is, makes it as far as the fifth inning and then leaves.

I have to admit, at least to myself, that I am glad Marcus arrives tomorrow. Laurie left a message that he should be here at 3:00 P.M., so I just have to stay alive until then. I should be able to manage that.

I will leave it up to Marcus to decide how to handle Stokan; Marcus is outstanding at stuff like that.

Before I go to bed, I go on Facebook. The Tara Foundation has a page, so I like to see posts from people that have adopted dogs from us, showing off their new family members.

There's nothing of consequence on there, so I go to my main page. There's never anything enlightening there, since I have so few Facebook friends, and this time is no exception. There's a post saying, "Share if you still eat sauerkraut." I have no idea if that means I should share the post or share the sauerkraut, so I log out of Facebook.

I double-lock the door and go to sleep. I wake up three or four times during the night because I hear noises, but each time everything seems okay, and my glances out into the parking lot don't reveal the truck.

I'm tired when I wake up in the morning, and the temptation to stay in bed, or at least in the safety of the room, is strong. But I am Andy Carpenter, fearless lawyer, so I have my morning coffee and muffin and head out to face the world.

My first stop is the Senator hotel in Augusta, not far from the state capitol and the Augusta General Hospital and Medical Center. The Senator was actually recommended to me as a nice place to stay, but it was too far from the Wiscasset courthouse to make sense.

I'm here to talk to Ginny Lawson, a radiology technician at the hospital who was a coworker and friend of Tina Welker's. Ginny was one of the people that the police interviewed, so that's why I picked her to talk to.

She didn't ask my role in the case; I just told her that I was investigating it. She was fine with that; it seems like she just wants to talk. She suggested we meet at the Senator for coffee, but as is my normal procedure, I'm going to inhale a blueberry muffin as well.

I can't say I'm expecting much from this interview; it's more like I'm doing due diligence and checking a box. If one of the victims of the murder was specifically being targeted, it seems more likely it was Charkin, because of his drug use.

Tina Welker has so far come across as a decent, fun-loving type who did not seem to have any serious enemies. I haven't done a deep dive into her life, but neither have I seen any red flags that would lead me in her direction.

I've gotten here first, so when a young woman walks in and

looks around, I wave to her. I've had little success in my life waving to young women, but this time this one sees me and realizes who I am.

We chitchat a bit about whether I like being in Maine. I tell her that I like it a lot, which I do, though I don't add that my working here makes me long for the day I can head home.

I'm about to move the conversation to where I want it to be when she says, "You wanted to talk about Tina? I told the police a long time ago that I didn't know anything."

Her unsolicited denial gives me some faint hope that she does know something. "In a matter this serious, it's good to go over things again. What was your relationship with Tina?"

"We were great friends, both at work and outside of it."

"Where do you work?"

"Augusta General . . . it's a big hospital not far from here."

I nod. "I passed it on the way. What do you do there?"

"I'm in radiology; so was Tina. We do mostly radiation treatment for cancer patients. She was actually the leader in our area. And she interacted with other units in the hospital who needed radiological services of all kinds done. Tina was a people person, so it was natural that she would assume that role." Then, "I still miss her, though had she lived she probably wouldn't still be working there."

"Why not?"

"A new director came in around the time Tina died and ruined everything. All these stupid rules, and she's been bringing in her own staff. Tina's replacement has alienated many of us. I might leave soon myself; I just feel like I should help them get through the machine changeover; it's going to be chaos, especially for the patients."

Ginny's job dissatisfaction isn't high on my list of concerns right now, so I go through the standard questions, asking if Tina had any enemies that Ginny knew of, or if Tina expressed any fear of anyone.

"I can't picture anyone not liking Tina," Ginny says, echoing what I've heard from everyone else. "But there's no question that she was acting weird those last few weeks, and she was unhappy."

"What do you mean by weird?"

"Maybe weird is too strong. But she stopped wanting to go out; we all used to have dinner together once or twice a week, and Tina backed out the last few times. That was unlike her, and it made those dinners a lot less enjoyable; that's for sure. We didn't laugh nearly as much."

"But you don't know why?"

"No, she never said, and I didn't want to pry. I know Tina's mother was real sick around that time, and money was a problem. Also might have been that guy she was seeing, but I can't be sure."

"Peter Charkin?"

Ginny nods. "Yeah, the guy who also died that day. He was no good for her; he changed her."

"Changed her how?"

"Her whole attitude; the way she looked at the world . . . the way she interacted with people. She seemed wary and maybe afraid. And he was controlling, which surprised me. Tina wasn't the type a guy could control. I remember hoping she'd dump him and get back to being Tina."

"Did she ever say anything specific? Maybe something he asked her to do? Or something he had done that bothered her?"

"No. Nothing that she ever mentioned."

"So when you heard she had died, you thought it might have something to do with him?"

"No. It was a random robbery. That's what the police said, right?"

"We're trying to figure that out. So Tina was also unhappy at work in those final weeks?"

Ginny nods. "Yeah. The place became a lot less fun."

I don't ask why radiating cancer patients is usually fun. And while I'm sympathetic to her being disgruntled at work, it doesn't relate to my case. "But Tina hadn't quit, had she?"

"No, she might have, if . . ." Ginny gets quiet for a few moments, then, "What a terrible day. Somehow even now it doesn't seem real. And she was tied to the chair like that; she must have been so scared. How could someone do that?"

Ginny pauses. I think she is going to burst into tears. But she keeps it together and says, "I'm just glad they caught the animal that did it."

If this is the prevailing sentiment in the community, and I'm afraid it is, I am not looking forward to jury selection.

New England, and Maine in particular, has got to be the center of the craft beer universe.

Until I got here, I didn't even know that craft beer had its own universe. But the bar at King Eider's, and I assume at every other bar around here, has an endless supply of beers that I have never heard of, but that everyone drinks.

The other night I ordered a Bud Light and I felt like everybody was staring at me.

This morning I have come to the source, or at least one of them. It's called the Maine Lighthouse Brewing Company. I assume it got the name because Maine seems weirdly proud of a bunch of lighthouses that it possesses, although this brewery is in Warren and not near any of them.

I'm not here to gulp my troubles away; I'm here to see the owner of the place, Mike Mitchell. Mitchell is identified in the discovery documents as a former boyfriend of Tina Welker's. Because of that status, he was immediately on police radar as a potential suspect, but like everyone else, the fact that his DNA was different from the blood found on the scene cleared him. He had willingly given a sample when the police requested it.

I had called Mitchell a few days ago, and though he said he had no desire to "relive" the horrible events, he agreed to speak with me. It's a large building, but with minimal office space. I assume there are large brewing rooms because the sign outside lists eleven different beers that Maine Lighthouse makes.

While I sometimes drink beer, I don't understand the appeal. It doesn't taste particularly good; at its best that taste is inoffensive. It's like coffee for me: I drink it because it's sort of the thing to do, and other people are drinking it too.

I tried a craft beer the other night, but that was a onetime deal that will not be repeated. It basically tasted like beer times twelve, and as I said, I don't even like beer times one.

Mitchell comes out into the reception area to greet me and, after doing so, asks, "You want the tour?"

I don't want the tour, but I don't want to insult him, so I hesitate. He fills the silence by saying, "Come on, I'll give you a quick one."

We enter an enormous room filled with giant metal vats. Despite his promise that the tour will be a "quick one," he goes on endlessly about barley and hops and all kinds of other beer words, showing me the process and what each vat is for. He also tells me there is another room the same size that has the same function.

I'm sure it's fascinating, but I basically couldn't care less. I feel like I should ask a question, so I come up with "What's the difference between a craft beer and a noncraft one?"

"Excellent question." I have a feeling he would have described my question as "excellent" had I asked where the bathroom is. "For one thing, to be classified as craft, less than six million barrels can be produced per year."

"So the goal is to graduate from craft to regular beer, meaning you sell more of it?"

He smiles. "No, we're happy where we are. There are other differences. Craft beer companies cannot be owned by the huge brewers, and craft beers are made by people who love beer. It's like wine in that respect."

"And each one of your eleven brands is different?"

"Absolutely."

"You could identify them in a blind taste test?"

He laughs. "Without question. And I do, much too frequently. Come on, let's go in my office."

We sit down in his office, a small, modest one that has a messy, worked-in look. "Sorry for the long-winded speech in there; I was probably trying to delay having this conversation."

"Sorry about that, but if I can ask questions now, I might not have to ask them in court." That was my not so subtle way of telling him that he needs to be forthcoming, or he'll have to be under oath.

"I understand."

"You dated Tina Welker?"

He nods. "On and off. We actually stopped seeing each other just a few months before she died. We remained friends; whether it would have stayed that way or not, I don't know."

"Why did you split up?"

"That sort of implies that we were together, and that's not really accurate. I was one of the people that Tina dated; she was open about it."

"Did that bother you?"

"Less than you would think. Probably because she was so upfront about it. Those were her terms and she stated them clearly. If the people she dated weren't good with that, they could move on."

"So you moved on?"

"I did. I was getting to the point where I wanted to settle down with someone, and Tina made it clear that wasn't going to be her. Like I say, everything was out in the open."

"Did you know Peter Charkin?"

"I did. We all went to high school together. And then Peter came to work for me here, at least for a while."

"Was Tina part of this high school group as well?"

He smiles. "Prom queen. Tina was really something." He pauses for a while, maybe revisiting a memory, then adds, "May she rest in peace."

"Were she and Charkin dating?"

Mitchell nods. "Definitely. By the time she died, I think she was dating him exclusively, which was unlike her. I certainly could never get her to be exclusive to me. I was one of a long list of guys who failed in that regard."

I had seen photos of Tina in the discovery documents. She was clearly attractive, although I also saw the coroner's photos after she was shot in the head, and those are pretty hard to get out of my mind.

"You said Charkin worked for you 'for a while.' Was he working here at the time he was killed?"

"No. He had left a few weeks before."

"Why?"

Mitchell hesitates, apparently measuring his words. "Let's say that he did not leave voluntarily."

"Which means you fired him."

"Reluctantly; he was a close friend."

"Why did you do it?"

"Peter was becoming somewhat unstable. I suspected drug use and I tried to talk with him, but I got nowhere. Eventually, his hours and his behavior became far too erratic, and it left me no choice."

"Did you have a sense as to where he was getting the drugs?"

"No. Honestly, maybe I should have tried to figure it out, but it didn't matter to me. Like I said, he was my friend, but firing him was a business decision. Actually, it wasn't really a decision at all. Once I realized he wasn't going to change what he was doing, I had no choice. It was hurting morale among the other employees."

"When you first heard that he and Tina were killed, did anyone come to mind that you thought could have done it?"

Mitchell grimaces at the memory. "What an awful day that was. But, no, no one came to mind. It was inconceivable to me that anyone I knew, anyone we knew, could have done something like that."

"Do the names Jerry Donnelly or Henry Stokan mean anything to you?"

"No, I don't think so. Should they?"

"Probably not. Thanks for your time and the beer education."

"No problem. You want some souvenir samples?"

"No thanks; no refrigerator in the hotel. But I'll get through them one at a time."

Marcus arrives at the hotel at 3:00 P.M.

Not 2:59, or 3:01. We all know people who are chronically late, and some who don't feel comfortable unless they arrive at places early. Not Marcus; he arrives exactly on time. Every time.

Marcus just nods when he sees me, which is just as well. I can never understand a single word that Marcus says, though he says so little that I have few opportunities to practice. Laurie understands him perfectly, which leaves me bewildered every time.

I've checked him in already; he'll occupy the room next to mine. So I have his key and take him upstairs to tell him the lay of the land. He has just one bag; I pick it up, but it's remarkably heavy, so I put it back down. "Do you have your rock collection in there?"

He doesn't answer, just picks the bag up as if it is filled with air. I got him a suite as well, though smaller than mine because Laurie and the dogs will be with me. He looks at the room and doesn't say a word. He sits at the table and says something that sounds like either "Stokan" or "Stmph" or something else entirely.

I'm going to go with Stokan since I'm not currently afraid of anyone named Stmph.

We sit at the table and I show Marcus the photo of Stokan. "Stokan," I say cleverly. For some reason when I'm with Marcus I tend to speak as few words as he does, though I try to make mine decipherable.

He looks at the photo and nods, then looks back at me.

"Has Laurie told you about him? That he threatened me?"

That draws an affirmative nod.

"I don't know if he just doesn't like out-of-town lawyers defending someone who might have killed two locals, or if he is somehow involved with our case. But last night I'm pretty sure he was in the parking lot with his friend, waiting for me to get here. I snuck in through the back."

Marcus doesn't say anything, which is not exactly a news event.

"Laurie will be here tomorrow. Until then I think your time is better spent helping me investigate; there are things you can do. You don't have to watch out for me. I'll be careful, and if I see Stokan again, I can call you."

"Nunnh."

I know from past experience that he means "no," and it's confirmed by his shake of the head. I also know where it's coming from: Laurie has sent him here to protect me, and that's what he's going to do. I guess there are worse ways for him to spend his time.

"Okay, I'm glad we cleared that up. Why don't you rest up and we'll go out to dinner? They've got great lobster rolls, if you like them."

I don't mention that the restaurant I'm taking him to is where Stokan approached me in the parking lot. Maybe I'll tell him later, or maybe not. I know Marcus well enough to know that it wouldn't matter; if he sees Stokan and has to deal with him, Marcus will deal with him.

I head back to my room. I have to admit that I'm not looking forward to dinner. When I'm with Marcus, I feel the need to carry the conversation, even though he clearly has no interest in it, and I'm incapable of it.

Marcus makes me nervous, even though he has demonstrated many times that he is on my side.

When we get to King Eider's, we sit at the bar, which gives me other people to talk to. The game on the television is a national ESPN game, Cardinals versus Cubs; the Red Sox are not playing tonight. But there is less conversation than usual; the scary and silent Marcus is an inhibiting factor.

Marcus probably couldn't talk even if he wanted to. We keep ordering lobster rolls and Marcus keeps eating them; it's as if his mouth is on the end of a lobster roll conveyer belt. I swear the kitchen staff in the back must have a pool going about how many he will eat. He eats seven of them by my count, though I could be missing one.

When we leave, I look around warily for any sign of Stokan. I don't see him or his truck, but that doesn't surprise me. He knows where I am staying and, unless he's a complete moron, probably has the back door covered this time.

Sure enough, when we get back to the inn, he and his large friend are in the truck, lights on and waiting for me. I point him out to Marcus, who doesn't say anything. It's possible he still has lobster roll in his mouth.

We get out and Marcus takes a step in the direction of Stokan's truck, rather than the front door of the inn.

"Marcus, wait." He stops. "I don't think we should confront him yet. Maybe we can get a better sense of what he wants, and whether he's working for anyone. Then we'll have a better chance of learning something."

Marcus just looks at me and doesn't say anything.

"Marcus, if he tries anything, we can deal with him. If not, let's wait. Okay?"

Again he doesn't answer. I'm not sure if he's going to do what I say. Laurie may have told him to deal with Stokan head-on.

I feel compelled to add, "If he's going to do something, he'll do it. Right now he's either just keeping an eye on me or trying to scare me by letting me know he's here."

Still no answer from Marcus or movement in either direction. Finally he gives a small nod and we head for the lobby door.

"You'll get your chance, Marcus. That I can promise you. Starting tomorrow, we change the rules."

I am looking forward to seeing my family.

Laurie called me after she dropped Ricky off at the camp bus and was starting her drive here. I got to speak to Ricky early this morning and told him I wished I could be there to see him off.

I could hear the excitement in his voice. He was looking forward to getting to camp to be with his friends, and then spending the summer playing sports and having no responsibilities other than having a good time.

I want to go to camp.

I discussed with Laurie my plan for Marcus, which I had gone over with him last night. We've been playing defense with Stokan, being protective and waiting to see where he would turn up.

We're turning that on its head. Instead of watching me, Marcus is going to watch Stokan. That might lead him back to me, since Stokan seems to be spending a lot of time following me. I've asked Sam Willis to find out where Stokan lives, so Marcus can locate him. Sam will have no trouble doing that, especially since he has the license plate number of Stokan's truck.

That would still leave Marcus on the scene and in position to protect me, should Stokan try anything. But if Stokan is working for somebody else in this situation, then he might lead Marcus to that person. We could then turn around and try to tie that person to our case. It's a long shot, for sure, but at least it's a shot.

The only risk in this new plan is if Stokan is not the only one following me. If another potential assailant is out there, Marcus wouldn't be tracking him and couldn't protect me from him. That person could then grab me and slit my throat without Marcus there to intervene.

That would be an unfortunate outcome.

I should be safe today, since I will be at the FBI offices in Portland. Laurie has talked to our friend Cindy Spodek, the number two agent in the Boston office, who has in turn set up this meeting. It's with Special Agent Donald Nichols, who has agreed to speak with me as a favor to her.

He only keeps me waiting for ten minutes, an all-time low in my FBI experience. That's a good sign; the not-so-good part comes when he opens our meeting by saying, "I've heard a lot about you."

"Let me guess; Cindy Spodek said I was a pain in the ass."

He nods. "Before she even said hello."

"She's quite a kidder, but that is a totally undeserved reputation. I am as user-friendly as they come. And I'm just looking for some information."

"About Jerry Donnelly. Cindy told me; that's why I took the meeting."

"I take it you're familiar with him?"

"Very."

"He's a bad guy?"

"Very."

"I was hoping for a little more specificity."

"Then you're going to need to tell me what your interest is in this."

"Fair enough. I'm defending Matt Jantzen, who was arrested for a double murder that took place two years ago."

Nichols nods. "I'm aware."

"So far it's fair to say that I'm casting a wide net, which means I'm blundering around hoping to bang into a clue. One of the victims, Peter Charkin, was into illegal drugs, so I'm attempting to find out if that drug use is connected to the crime."

"Where does Jerry Donnelly come in?"

"I'm told that that Jerry Donnelly is the dominant player when it comes to drug sales in Maine."

"Certainly true enough."

"How ruthless and violent is Donnelly?"

"Very ruthless and very violent."

"So if someone like Charkin owed Donnelly money and wouldn't pay, would he react by killing him and his girlfriend?"

Nichols shakes his head. "First of all, Donnelly has people that handle the sales for him; he doesn't stand on street corners or make collection calls. But let's say that this Charkin guy stiffed Donnelly's people; killing would not be a first step. Not even a second step and maybe not a third.

"First he'd threaten him, and then he'd have people break his legs. Donnelly would not find it productive to kill a customer, not without trying other options. He needs customers these days."

"What about if it was not just a matter of collections? What if Charkin was trying to do something like move in on his territory?"

"Different story," Nichols says. "If Charkin was dumb enough to do that, and very few people would be that dumb, Donnelly wouldn't hesitate to kill him. But he wouldn't do it in a way that would help your case."

"What do you mean?"

"Well, my understanding is that your client's DNA was at the scene. I assume you will claim that it was somehow planted there. If Charkin was moving in on him, Donnelly wouldn't play it like that. He'd want to send a message that he's not to be messed with. Framing your client defeats that purpose."

"Well, I'm definitely not going to pick you for the jury. The people that handle his street action, how do I find out which one would cover that area of the Midcoast?"

"I'll try to find that out for you. Give me your phone number."

I do so. "Do you know Henry Stokan?"

"Yeah, I know him."

"Is he one of Donnelly's salesmen?"

"No, he's hired muscle. Very dangerous and very stupid. Do not go anywhere near him."

"He threatened me. Might that be on Donnelly's behalf?"

Nichols nods. "Very possibly. Have you given him a different reason?"

"Not that I know of."

"Most visitors to our state don't make enemies quite this fast."

I nod. "It's part of my charm."

There has never been a better-looking group to exit a car.

I'm not talking about recently, or in my experience. I'm talking about in the entire history of cars.

I'm in the parking lot when Laurie arrives with Tara, Sebastian, and Hunter. I've been waiting out here for a half hour because I wanted to see them at the first possible time.

I haven't seen Laurie in almost two weeks and, boy, has she aged well. I can also confirm that she has also not lost any of her hugging ability; if the dogs weren't barking, I would never let this one end.

I spend the next five minutes hugging and petting Tara, Sebastian, and Hunter. Hunter looks comfortable and at home with his temporary stepsiblings; his tail is wagging every bit as hard as theirs.

I bring the entire crew up to what will be our home for the duration of the case. Laurie seems to like the room; it's more spacious than she expected. The dogs set about testing out the furniture and carpeting to decide where they will be most comfortable sleeping.

I go outside to get the bags and bring them in. Laurie wedged more stuff into this car than could fit in the average tractor trailer.

I had made a stop at PetSmart yesterday for dog dishes and dog food, so all of this stuff is Laurie's.

If Matt Jantzen gets convicted and is sentenced to forty years in prison, Laurie will be able to visit him every day for that time in a different outfit. The strange thing is that nine out of ten days she wears jeans; I think she just likes having the other options. The chance that I will have the guts to question her about it is somewhere in the area of absolute zero.

I'm bringing in food tonight, and Marcus is going to join us. He will update us on his day spent trailing Stokan, and I'll describe the progress I've made so far. Neither of those things will take a long time.

After that we can plot our next moves. The trial is a ways off, but trials are like the images in passenger-side mirrors; they are always closer than they seem.

When Laurie and I are done with dinner, Marcus is, of course, still eating. Laurie and I take the dogs for a walk in a grassy area near the inn. It's a short stroll, but if we walk to Connecticut, Marcus will still be eating when we get back.

I could do the walk with the three dogs by myself, but Laurie insists on coming along. I'm sure it is so she can provide protection should Stokan appear on the scene. Laurie is not Marcus, but she protects well.

When we get back, Marcus describes his day following Stokan. Weirdly, Stokan led him to Boston, to Fenway Park. They arrived just before the Red Sox game, and Stokan went in. Marcus didn't follow; instead he watched Stokan's car.

Stokan left and went back to the car fifteen minutes after he went in; the game was still in the first inning. When he got back to Maine, he tracked me down and started following me again. He obviously didn't try anything, and therefore Marcus did not intervene.

Marcus is in favor of dealing with Stokan more directly, but Laurie agrees with me that it is better to wait, so Marcus reluctantly goes along with it.

Stokan is becoming increasingly interesting to me. His stalking me is way beyond casual; the time he is putting in definitely seems to indicate that he has some serious involvement here. I have no idea why that is the case, or whether he is self-motivated or working for someone else. But we had better find out.

I have not done anywhere near a full investigation into Tina Welker's life, but I've learned nothing to make me believe that she was the intended target of the killings. It's more likely that it was Charkin, because of the drug connection.

There also remains the definite possibility that it was random, and that would be a disaster for our defense. But I doubt it's the case: random killers doing home invasion robberies do not generally bring along a vial of someone else's blood to leave on the scene.

Laurie is going to pick up the investigation into Tina Welker. She will talk to more of Tina's friends and work colleagues. Many of them will be reluctant to talk to people representing the person they believe is her killer, and Laurie is more likely to get them to open up.

I'll focus on Charkin and the potential source of his illegal drugs, possibly including Jerry Donnelly. I'll also see what I can find out about the neighbor that Tina Welker was concerned about, according to her friend Rachel Manning. She said that she thought his name was something like Bennett, and I had Sam Willis confirm that, in addition to getting me the address where he lives and works.

There is always the chance that some demented guy, possibly the neighbor, committed this awful act. But then again, we run up against the not-credible possibility that he brought along a little jar of Matt Jantzen's blood with him.

So that is the plan, such as it is.

Marcus goes back to his room. Laurie and I have a glass of wine, surrounded by three sleeping, contented dogs. It would be even nicer if Ricky was here, but I know he's having a hell of a lot more fun with his friends at camp.

"Did you miss me?" I ask.

Laurie looks confused. "Did you go somewhere?"

"I came here, to Maine, and you couldn't handle it, so you followed me, displaying a pathetic lack of independence."

She smiles. "Okay. I missed you." Then, "Did you miss me?"

I stand up and hold out my hand. "Let's put it this way. I would give up lobster rolls for you."

Roy Bennett?"

A large man in overalls and boots is coming out of his house. It's two doors down from Tina Welker's Nobleboro home, where the murders took place. Bennett is the man that Rachel Manning said Tina Welker had some concerns about.

I've just pulled up in front of this house as he's coming out. He looks at me suspiciously, so I give him my winning Andy Carpenter smile.

He continues to look at me suspiciously. "Who are you?" he asks, without identifying himself.

"My name is Andy Carpenter. Can I speak with you for a couple of minutes?"

"What about?"

This is a guy who answers questions with questions, something that gets on my nerves when I'm not the one doing it. "I'm investigating the murders that took place in that house two years ago." I point to Tina's house, just in case murders are commonplace on this street.

"I got nothing to say about it."

"It won't take long."

"It won't happen at all because I got nothing to say. I just told you that."

I walk toward him, maintaining my smile. "See, here's the thing, Roy. I'm a lawyer, so I went to law school, which means I know the law. Just like you work in a lumberyard, so you know lumber. So the law says that if you don't talk to me willingly, I can go down to Masters Lumber Yard this afternoon, walk right in, and serve you a subpoena. That means you will have to leave work and talk to me under oath in front of a judge. You understand?"

What I am saying is total bullshit. Bennett should know that; they probably even taught it in lumber school. But I can see a flash of worry on his face, which means he is probably buying the garbage I'm selling.

"How long will this take? I've got to get to work."

"Just a few minutes."

"We need to go inside?"

I have no desire to get into a closed, indoor space with this guy. "No, we can talk right here. I can lean against my car, and you can lean against yours."

He grudgingly nods and walks toward me. Up close he's even larger than I thought, and I thought he was large. "I don't know nothing about that murder. Just what I read in the paper."

"I understand." The truth is that I'm not here to accuse him; I just want to get a sense of the guy to determine if he deserves a place on our skimpy suspect list. "Were you home the night that it happened?"

"Yeah, I was home."

"Did you see or hear anything suspicious?"

"No."

"What about visitors that she had in the days before she died? Did you notice anyone that seemed concerning?"

He snorts a laugh. "She had plenty of visitors."

"Men?"

"Oh, yeah."

"So she went out with a lot of different men?"

"That's for damn sure. She wasn't too damn particular."

"If you don't mind my asking, did you ever go out with her?"
I know from Rachel Manning that Tina shot him down.

"A working guy like me? No way."

"So she wasn't particular about men, but she still wouldn't
go out with you?" I'm trying to piss him off, just a little, to see
how he reacts. If we were inside, I probably wouldn't have the
guts to do it.

"What's that supposed to mean?" he asks, throwing in a bit
of a snarl.

"Which part didn't you understand, Roy?" I don't wait for
an answer; it was just more of an effort to goad him. "Did Tina
even talk to you, or did she ignore you?"

"You know something? I didn't like her; she had a hot-shit
attitude. And I don't like you either."

"What do you do when you don't like someone?"

"In your case, you don't want to find out."

"Have you ever spent any time in prison, Roy?"

He doesn't answer; just looks like he is about to hit me. I bring
out that look in a lot of people, and I'm not fond of the look.
I'm scared he is going to do something I might regret.

I open my car door, and as I'm getting in, I say, "Nice talking
with you."

As I'm driving away, I wait for my heart to stop pounding
and then reflect on the conversation. There are people that I
would say could never commit a murder. Laurie, for example.
Mother Teresa would be another.

Roy Bennett is no Mother Teresa.

Does the name Danny McCaskill mean anything to you?"

Charlie Tilton thinks for a while and shrugs. "Outfielder for the Cardinals?"

"Member of the militia here in Maine," I say.

He snaps his fingers. "Damn . . . that was my next guess." Then, "Just kidding; I read the discovery. But, no, I never heard of him before that. I did represent a militia guy once, but it had nothing to do with his membership in any group. He had allegedly robbed a liquor store; the jury deliberated for an hour and a half before removing the word *allegedly.* So I know a bit about them, but I'm not familiar with McCaskill, other than what was in the discovery."

According to that discovery, the police had at least a minor interest in McCaskill during the initial murder investigation, because of some connection to Charkin. But they apparently lost that interest pretty quickly. I suppose that was a result of the DNA not matching up. "Are militias big here in Maine?"

Another shrug. "I don't think more so than any other rural kind of state, but we have them. But a lot of people here like their guns, and they like their freedom, and they're always sure that one or both of them are going to be taken away. But when you ask about Maine . . . I'm not sure that's the right question."

"What do you mean?"

"Well, one of the growing problems, as I understand it, is that the militant militia groups are not interested in borders. They are grouping together across states to become bigger and more powerful."

"Where do they get their financing?"

"Financing?"

"Yeah. They buy guns, they serve lunch at militia meetings . . . where are they getting the money for all that?"

"That's another problem; they're often extraordinarily well funded. People with big money who share their beliefs, but don't want to get gunpowder on their hands, manage to get money to them."

"Rich idealogues?"

Charlie nods. "Yes, but sometimes economics rears its ugly head. Chaos means big money if you're on the right side."

"What does that mean?"

"Every negative event, especially the violent ones, provokes a reaction. When 9/11 happened, you think that hurt the defense contractors, or the metal-scanner manufacturers? When the pandemic happened and people were stuck inside, you think Amazon and Netflix suffered?"

I nod. "Makes sense."

"Right. Some of these groups, not all of them by any means, want to overthrow the world. There are rich people ready to take advantage of that, and profit from it. And then there are rich people who just think it's a good idea."

"Depressing."

"You have any reason to suspect McCaskill, beyond the fact that the police considered him?"

"None whatsoever."

"That's as good a reason as any. You going to try and interview him?"

"As soon as I leave here."

"He expecting you?"

I shake my head. "No, I'm going to try his house first, and if he's not there, I'll find him at work."

"Where does he work?"

"I have no idea. He's a landscaper, so I'll just search for lawns and plants and stuff. I'll deal with that if he's not home. It's raining, so maybe he'll take the day off."

"Being alone with a militia guy in his house and implying that he might be guilty of murder might not be the smartest thing to do."

"You want to come along?"

Charlie thinks for a few moments. "I guess so. I've got to protect you; you're my meal ticket."

"It's nice to be appreciated. Let's go."

I have to admit that I'm pleased Charlie is going with me. I had even considered bringing Marcus along, but I'd rather he keep an eye on Stokan. "Hold on a few minutes; I need to make a phone call."

I call Sam Willis, who as always answers on the first ring. "Sam, there's a guy named Danny, or Daniel, McCaskill. He lives in Jefferson, Maine."

"What do you want to know about him?"

"I'm going to see him; I should be there in about twenty minutes, maybe twenty-five." I look over at Charlie questioningly to see if I have the timing right, and he nods that I do. "When I leave there, I want to know if he calls anyone. Monitor his calls for the next couple of days."

"You got it."

"There's a chance he won't be there and I won't get to speak to him. I'll call you back if that happens."

"I'm on it. You in any danger up there? I could come up and work backup."

Sam wants to be much more than an accountant and a computer guy; he wants to be able to shoot people. "That's okay, Sam. Marcus is here."

"Oh. He should be able to handle it, but if he needs help, I'm a phone call away."

"I'll mention that to him." I hang up.

Charlie asks, "What the hell was that about? How will this guy Sam know who McCaskill calls?"

"He breaks into the phone company computers. You want him to mark your phone bill as paid?"

"I don't think what he's doing is legal."

"Really? I cut class the day they went over legalities in law school."

Charlie looks a bit troubled by this, so I add, "Here's the deal. I never have Sam get anything I can't eventually get myself through a legal subpoena, and if I want to present anything in court, that's what I do. This way I have it in real, actionable time."

"You hotshot New York lawyers are really something."

"New Jersey."

"Whatever."

The cold, driving rain has gotten heavier during the drive to McCaskill's house.

Along the way I ask Charlie to work on challenging the DNA evidence, to try to find some flaw in the collection, chain of custody, or maintenance. If we are ultimately going to get anywhere, we are going to have to deal with the prosecution's evidentiary contention that Matt's blood was at the scene.

"Can I hire an expert if it gets to that?" Charlie asks. "Someone, unlike me, who knows what he or she is talking about?"

"Yes."

"You don't shy away from spending money; I'll give you that. Can I have a raise?"

"No."

"What are you running, a sweatshop?"

McCaskill lives in Jefferson near Damariscotta Lake. Everybody in Maine lives near a lake; lakes are as ubiquitous as lobster rolls.

We run from the car to McCaskill's front porch, which fortunately has an overhang that protects us from the rain. I ring the bell, but no one answers. I ring it again, and after a brief wait someone opens the door.

It's a big guy, wearing jeans and a T-shirt that simply says UNITY. He's wearing socks, but no shoes. "Yeah?"

"Daniel McCaskill?"

"Yeah?" He's quite a conversationalist.

"We'd like to ask you some questions."

"What about?"

"A police matter," I say, deceiving but not lying. "Can we come in?"

"You cops?"

"We're officers of the court." Again, technically true, though I can feel Charlie staring at me. It's possible I hired a lawyer with integrity; I might need to adjust my screening criteria. "Now can we come in? We'd rather ask the questions here than at the precinct." Once again, I speak the technical truth, though I don't mention that I don't have the authority to bring him anywhere near the precinct.

McCaskill frowns and opens the door wider, a heartwarming, welcoming gesture if ever I have seen one. I motion *After you* to Charlie. He does go first, but seems less than thrilled about it.

We walk into what I guess serves as the den. The room is a mess: clothing and papers strewn all over, on the floor and furniture. He is either a slob or he's in the middle of spring dirtying. McCaskill sits on the couch, but both Charlie and I independently decide to stand.

"So?"

I don't think McCaskill's asking whether we'd like something to drink. As far as being a welcoming host, he makes Tina Welker's neighbor Roy Bennett look positively gracious.

"Peter Charkin was an associate of yours?" I ask.

He groans; an actual, audible groan. "Is that what this is about? Charkin? I thought they caught the guy."

"We're just doing background work, filling in the holes in the case. Someone has, in fact, been charged with the crime and is awaiting trial."

"Good. I hope they fry the bastard. So what do you want with me?"

I notice Charlie walk a few steps to the right and take a seat on a couch. I'm surprised that he does that; he literally has to move papers and wrappings to the side.

"We're examining Mr. Charkin's involvement in the group known as the Liberators. We believe you can help us with that."

"Yeah? Well, I can't help you with that."

Charlie interjects; he's now gotten up from a short stay on the sofa. "How long have you been a member?"

"I got nothing to say about that." McCaskill then immediately contradicts himself. "You got a problem with people who care about this country?"

"No one said anything about a problem," I say. "We are just trying to determine what Charkin's role was."

"His role?"

I nod. "Right. In the Liberators. Commanding officer, chief cook and bottle washer, social secretary . . . that kind of thing. What was his job?"

"He was a patriot."

"Is that time-consuming work?"

"You a wiseass?"

I nod. "Yes. Pretty much."

McCaskill stands up. If there's a way to stand up slowly, but aggressively, he pulls it off. "You two get out of my house now. You got ten seconds, or you're going to get carried out."

This is not feeling like an empty threat; I can tell by the shaking of my legs. I nod to Charlie and start for the door.

"Thanks for your time," Charlie says.

McCaskill doesn't follow us; we are apparently meant to let ourselves out.

We don't talk until we're in the car. Then Charlie says, "You make a lot of friends, do you?"

"I'm usually more charming than I was in there."

"Osama bin Laden was usually more charming than you were in there."

"I wasn't trying to cajole him into a confession. I was trying to see if he had a temper, a short fuse, if he was capable of violence."

"I would go with 'D, all of the above.'"

"So now we add him to our suspect list."

"We have a suspect list?"

"We do. And it's getting bigger all the time."

Charlie reaches into his pocket and pulls out what looks like a plastic piece of packaging. "Your friend Sam might want this."

"What is it?"

"It's the packaging for a burner phone. I've got a feeling our boy McCaskill doesn't use phones in his name."

"How did you know what that was?"

Charlie shrugs. "Not all of my clients have been completely reputable."

I call Sam and read him the numbers off the packaging; it's all he will need to trace calls from that phone. "I'm on it," Sam says unnecessarily.

I hang up and turn to Charlie. "So that's why you sat down on that disgusting couch? So you could steal that wrapping?"

"I see it as taking one for the team."

"Charlie, you are my kind of lawyer."

"Can I have a raise?"

"Not a chance."

Dr. Robert Charkin is an optician in Thomaston, about twenty minutes from Damariscotta.

If you tied me down and threatened me with death, I couldn't tell you the difference between an optician, an optometrist, and an ophthalmologist. There might not even be a difference; now that I think of it, I've never seen them in the same room. Maybe the whole thing is an opti-scam.

I had called Charkin and told him that I wanted to talk to him about his murdered brother, Peter. I also said that while I was there, he could examine my eyes, since I've been finding myself squinting when I read.

Thomaston, like most Maine communities, is steeped in history and filled with old buildings. But Charkin's place of business, a storefront on the town's main street, is bright and white and incongruously modern.

I have a five-minute wait while Dr. Charkin is with a patient, so I look through a brochure on laser surgery. I have friends who have had it done and rave about it, but the idea that I will voluntarily allow someone to operate on my eyes with something that could cut through metal is a complete nonstarter.

When I get into his examining room, we shake hands.

"Did you really want an examination, or did you think that was the only way I would talk to you?"

"Examine away. We can talk afterwards, if that's okay."

He tells me to put my chin on a chin rest, which seems to be a logical place to put it. Then he looks at my eyes with a bright light and starts asking me which of two lenses allows me to see clearer.

He does it so many times that by the time he's finished I'm just guessing.

"Do I need glasses?"

"I would say that they would help you, at least for reading, yes."

"That wasn't the answer I was looking for. What's my problem?"

"You don't have a problem; it's a normal, age-related deterioration of vision. You're not getting any younger."

"How do you know that? Did you see me last year? You have nothing to compare it to. Maybe I am getting younger."

He smiles. "I'll write you a prescription, and as you get even younger, you can make your decision."

"You're not doing laser surgery on me."

"Very true. I don't do laser surgery. I'm an optometrist."

"Yeah, sure."

We head into his private office.

"So you want to talk about my brother?"

"I do. I am trying to understand who might have wanted to kill him."

"Other than your client."

"My client didn't know him. But if my client is guilty, then I'll come up empty in my search."

Charkin nods. "Okay. Ask away."

"Your brother was using opioids and was probably addicted. You were aware of that?"

"I was. I confronted him a number of times. Those confrontations accomplished nothing other than destroying, or at least badly damaging, our relationship."

"How long was he using?"

"Not sure. But at least a year, maybe longer."

"Do you know where he was getting them?"

Charkin shakes his head. "I do not. If I did, I would have already told the police."

"Do you know where he got the money to pay for them?"

"No; that's another mystery. I lent him money about a year before he died; that's why I said he was using drugs at least that long. He made up a story to get the money; it was all bull."

"The police found five thousand dollars in cash in his house."

Charkin nods. "I know; I wound up with it, because his will left everything to me. That was pretty much the extent of his possessions, other than his car."

"Any idea why he had it in cash like that? Or where he got it?"

"No idea. But needing money became a consuming theme for the last months of his life."

"He worked for his friend Mike Mitchell at the brewery."

"Yes. Mike kept him on longer than he probably should have, because of their friendship. With his addiction, Peter was something less than a reliable employee."

"You spoke to Mitchell about it at the time?"

"I did. He told me that he also confronted Peter about the drug use, with a similar lack of effectiveness."

"But it's possible your brother acquired drugs and was unable to pay for them?"

Charkin smiles. "Is that your theory? That he was murdered by a drug dealer over nonpayment?"

"I am on an endless quest to develop a theory."

"If that was the case, I would have thought that Peter would give up the five thousand dollars in cash rather than face death."

The guy makes sense, which is rather annoying. "Are you aware that your brother had a connection to a militia group?"

Charkin laughs, which surprises me. Then, "I know. It's completely bizarre."

"Why?"

"Those people have an ideology, a mission. I, and I assume you, think most of it is misguided, but it's real to them. That wasn't Peter. I loved him, he was my brother, but Peter did not want to change the world. Peter wanted to make the world more comfortable for Peter."

"But the connection was real. I've talked to them."

Charkin nods. "No question about it. But he wasn't interested in their cause. He was running some kind of scam, and it had to involve money. Whatever he might have been doing with them, he thought he had a way to profit from it. That was Peter."

"Did you know Tina Welker?"

"No, never met her. You think she was just in the wrong place at the wrong time with the wrong person?"

"Certainly possible. I'm working on a whole bunch of theories, hoping I'll hit on one that is right. You really think I need glasses?"

"Not urgently, but you're getting there. Youth is creeping up on you."

L aurie and I are settling into a routine.

During the day we are each working on the case; she has been interviewing more of Tina Welker's friends, while I have started on the Peter Charkin side.

Each morning we take the dogs for a walk and discuss what we'll be doing that day. Of course, we can't just leave the room; Laurie has to make the bed first.

The whole bed-making concept has always struck me as borderline bizarre. It is entirely unproductive. Once the bed is made, the next thing that will happen to it is that it will become unmade that night.

The entire unmaking process could be avoided by just not making it in the first place. It would be a win-win for lazy people everywhere.

But Laurie takes it to a bizarre level. The hotel employs people whose main function is to come in and make the bed every day. Yet since Laurie has already done it before they arrive, that person must think we sleep on the floor. Making a hotel bed is like washing a rental car; no one does it . . . besides Laurie.

To make matters even more ridiculous, Hunter considers it his solemn duty to burrow into the bedspread until he completely messes it up, making the bed unmade. He's trying to create a place he weirdly considers comfortable, but the net effect is that Laurie probably remakes the bed four times a day. I have to assume it pisses Hunter off each time.

Neither Tara nor I understand any of these behaviors, but since it doesn't affect our lives, we don't attempt to intervene. Instead, I go downstairs with the dogs while Laurie is making the bed. Tara, Sebastian, and Hunter have become favorites of both the guests and staff, so they hold court while we wait, accepting petting and biscuits.

I'm trying to incorporate writing letters to Ricky at camp into my day. I miss him terribly; it feels like I haven't seen him in years. I expect that he must have gray hair and a beard by now. But I'm not a great letter writer, so I have to discipline myself to keep up.

At night, Laurie and I either go to King Eider's for dinner or get takeout from there. Marcus hasn't wanted to join us, though he has a standing invitation. I know he's watching Stokan, but I would hope he takes time to eat.

Last night we were at King Eider's, and Laurie got something of a thrill. She noticed one of her favorite novelists, a guy named David Rosenfelt, having dinner in the next booth. He apparently lives near here.

She considered asking him for his autograph, but decided it would be too pushy to interrupt his meal. I don't get it, anyway. I tried reading one of his books and could barely get through fifty pages.

Tonight Laurie has gone there to pick up dinner; maybe she's hoping he'll be there again. I take the opportunity to walk Tara, Sebastian, and Hunter in the small park near the hotel. Laurie won't be happy about it because she wants to be with me on the nighttime walks in case I run into Stokan.

Or more accurately, in case he runs into me.

I'm feeling guilty that I haven't taken the dogs to any of the great dog-walking areas in town that people have told me about. I've just been too busy, but I need to carve out time. They will love it, and for some inexplicable reason, dog walking clears my head and helps me think.

There's no such thing as a quick walk with this crew because of Sebastian's plodding pace. Tara's used to it by now, but I think it annoys Hunter.

Tonight we walk for about five minutes into the park and then turn around. Getting Sebastian to reverse direction is akin to turning the *Queen Mary,* but I get it done.

Sebastian furthers delays us by pausing to do his business, and I lean over with my trusty plastic bag to remove all evidence of it. As I'm doing so, I hear a voice say, "Well, the piece of shit is picking up a piece of shit."

I can tell by the panic in my gut that I recognize the voice; it's Henry Stokan. That it's a surprisingly clever opening line doesn't quell my fear any.

I look up and see Stokan and the other large guy that was with him that night in the parking lot. It's dark and silent in this park, and if Marcus is around, he has not yet made his presence known. I sure hope he is.

Running is not an option, not with the dogs. And I sure as hell can't leave them behind with these two assholes; they might hurt them to send a message. Or worse.

"What is it you want? I gave the police your license plate number. If anything happens to me, they will come right for you."

"We sent you a message and you didn't listen," Stokan says. The two start moving toward me. Then, "Who the hell are you?"

I hadn't even realized it; he moves so quickly. But Marcus is standing between them and me. I don't know how Tara, Sebastian, and Hunter feel about it, but I am extraordinarily relieved.

Marcus doesn't answer the question because, if he doesn't speak to me, why should he speak to them? He just stands there, waiting.

"You got ten seconds to move out of the way, friend," Stokan says, even though I don't think he really considers Marcus his friend.

Marcus neither moves nor speaks, and the guy with Stokan, who will hereafter be referred to as "the idiot," says, "Let me take care of this." He says it with the confidence of someone who doesn't have a clue as to what the actual balance of power is.

He moves toward Marcus. In the dark it's hard to make out exactly what happens, but it doesn't take more than three or four seconds for the idiot to be prone in the grass, unconscious.

Stokan, clearly not a Rhodes scholar himself, is undaunted. He moves toward Marcus and starts punching. Strangely, all Marcus does is block the punches; he doesn't hit back. It's as if they are fencing with their arms, but Marcus has chosen to only parry, not thrust.

Stokan is getting nowhere and getting frustrated. Marcus is like Ali, playing rope-a-dope. There is no rope, but Stokan is clearly playing the part of dope.

Finally, with Stokan exhausted and at a loss for what to do, Marcus knocks his lights out with one quick right hand, followed by a left cross. It is beautiful to behold. Stokan lands on top of the idiot, and neither of them moves.

"I guess we showed them."

This does not prompt a response from Marcus.

Now all I have to do is figure out what to do. I want to question Stokan to try to find out why he has made it his mission to stalk me. That is not going to happen in the next few minutes, since he is currently unconscious.

"Marcus, I want to talk to him when he wakes up. I'm going to take the dogs to the hotel and come right back. If they wake up before I get back, which does not seem likely, please keep them here, okay?"

"Yunhh."

I take that as a yes and move toward the hotel as fast as Sebastian's fat little legs are willing to carry him, which is not very fast. When I get to the room, I quickly tell Laurie what has happened, and she heads back to the park with me.

Marcus is more prone to listening to Laurie than me. If he decides that he wants to do something to Stokan and the idiot, like crush their skulls, she would be able to dissuade him in a way that I could not.

Without Sebastian holding us back, we get out to the park and reach the scene quickly. The only problem is that no one is there. Marcus, Stokan, the idiot . . . they're all gone.

"Are you sure this is where you were?"

"I think so; I'm pretty sure. It's obviously dark, but . . . yes, I'm sure. Where the hell could they have gone?"

"There has to be a road near here. Stokan must have driven here, and Marcus must have as well. Maybe he took them somewhere."

We walk farther, and sure enough, Laurie is right. There's a road just behind the trees, and Stokan's truck is parked there. Marcus's car is nowhere to be found.

"You don't think he'll kill them, do you?"

"Not unless he has to defend himself. You think they'll attack him again?"

I shake my head. "They're stupid, but they can't be that stupid. I just hope they weren't already dead. They were just lying there; I didn't check to see if they were breathing."

"I guess we'll know when we know."

"What are we going to do now?"

"Go back, have dinner, and try to reach Marcus," she says. "But he'll show up whenever he's done doing what he's doing."

Sounds like a plan.

We're about an hour past dinner when the phone rings.

Laurie takes the call and I don't bother picking up the other extension for two reasons. One is that I wouldn't understand a word Marcus said anyway; I'd spend the entire conversation looking for subtitles. The other reason is that it's Laurie's cell phone, so there is no other extension. I could have her put it on speakerphone, but the first reason makes that unproductive.

Laurie asks a lot of questions, but she mostly listens and takes occasional notes. According to her, and I can't attest to this one way or the other, Marcus's investigative reports are generally complete and do not require much prodding or further explanation.

She finally hangs up. "That was Marcus."

"No kidding. What happened?"

"Well, they're alive. He took them somewhere else to question them. He wasn't clear on why, but said something about cars going by on the road. I guess he didn't want to be interrupted."

"Did he get anything out of them?"

She looks at me with a frown, as if it was a ridiculous question, which it was. "This is Marcus we're talking about. Of course he got information from them."

I wait for Laurie to continue.

"Stokan is working for Jerry Donnelly, but only indirectly. He's actually taking orders from one of Donnelly's lieutenants; apparently Donnelly delegates." Laurie looks at her notes. "The lieutenant's name is Carmody . . . Lyle Carmody."

"Does Carmody deal drugs for Donnelly?"

Laurie nods. "He does. Covers the whole county and neighboring Knox County as well. Donnelly apparently has quite an operation."

"So he was supplying Charkin?"

"That's the thing. According to Stokan, Charkin was not a customer. Stokan swears that's the case. He doesn't know where Charkin was getting his drug supply from, but it wasn't Carmody. He knows that because he does some collections and deliveries for Carmody, and he never saw Charkin.

"And Stokan says that if it wasn't Carmody, then it wasn't Donnelly, because Carmody has the exclusive on this area."

This isn't making sense. "So if Charkin wasn't getting drugs through Donnelly, but Stokan was indirectly working for Donnelly, why was Stokan after me?"

"Stokan swears that he doesn't know, that Carmody told him to scare you and rough you up a little bit. They want you to back off, but I'm not sure what it is you're supposed to back off of. It's hard to believe they think you'd resign the case."

"And Marcus believed him?"

"He did. Marcus has a way of providing incentive to cooperate."

I nod. "And if he gave up Donnelly's name, he'd give up everything. Naming Donnelly puts him in major jeopardy. From what we've heard about Donnelly, he wouldn't be likely to forgive and forget."

"There's obviously something else we're not understanding."

"I can see two possibilities. One is that we've turned over a rock with Donnelly under it, even though we have no idea which rock it was. Two is that Donnelly had another reason to kill Charkin that wasn't drug related."

"That five grand found in Charkin's house . . . you think he could have somehow stolen it from Donnelly?"

"Doesn't sound likely, but nothing else does either. . . . What did Marcus do with them when he was finished?"

"He told them that if he saw them within a mile of you again, he would kill them. I suspect they believed him. I don't know where he left them after that, but it doesn't much matter."

The evening's events have left me a little shaken, and I'm starting to feel it now. "Did you know there are lawyers who never get their lives threatened? We read about them in law school."

"Really? What boring lives they must lead."

"I can use a drink to calm my nerves. We have any craft beer?"

"No, but we have wine."

"That will have to do."

"Let's have a glass and then go to bed," she says. "I find daredevil lawyers to be wildly exciting."

take a different route on my morning walk with the dogs today.

I have a simple rule of thumb: if I go someplace where two huge thugs try to attack me on behalf of a violent drug dealer, I avoid that place for at least twenty-four hours. It's a tactic that has served me well.

This is a more crowded route, at least in terms of other people walking their own dogs. I have to stop a few times to let my dogs sniff the newly met strangers, and vice versa. That's fine with me, except it forces me to make small talk with their owners. I'm not a fan of small talk; I'm not that crazy about big talk either.

I get back, grab muffins for Laurie and me, and head upstairs for a shower. Laurie is not back yet. Because she doesn't have her exercise bike here, she goes for a run every morning. She runs three miles, and I would join her if I was in shape and insane.

As she is walking in, not even breathing heavily, my cell phone rings. The caller ID says that it's the US government calling, so I answer in my mature, adult voice, as befitting the occasion. "Hello?"

"Good morning, Mr. Carpenter, this is Agent Donald Nichols, FBI, Portland office. We spoke in my office earlier."

"I can remember that far back."

"I'd like to come up there to speak with you this morning."

"What about?"

"If I was inclined to discuss it on the phone, I wouldn't need to come up there."

That kind of logic is difficult to argue with, and I'm intrigued by why Nichols would be calling, so I agree to wait at the hotel for him. It's not a great concession, since I had no place to go anyway.

He says that he's in Brunswick and will be here in about forty minutes. I tell Laurie about the call, so she quickly takes a shower so that she can also hear what Nichols has to say.

Sam Willis calls to update me on his progress on the cyber-searches I gave him. "Let's start with McCaskill. In the day that you visited him, he made four calls. One was almost immediately after you left from the burner phone, the other three were that night. Two of the nighttime calls were from his regular phone; the other was from the burner.

"The two nighttime calls from the regular phone were probably insignificant. One was to his boss at the landscaping company, and another was to a pizza place. Unless people interesting to you work at either of those places, you can probably disregard them.

"The two burner calls, the morning one and another later that night, were to a guy named Gavin Helms. Helms is also using a burner phone."

"So how do you know it's him?"

"He was dumb enough to buy it with his credit card; the purchase was in northern Vermont. Anyway, I ran a search on Helms. He's got five arrests, two for assault, one for illegal assembly, and two for illegal possessions of outlawed firearms. He's got a media trail also; he's a member of a militia group called the Liberators."

That's the group that McCaskill belongs to, but I don't interrupt Sam to mention it.

"The other interesting thing about Helms is that he was a close associate of a man named Darrin Jeffrey. Do you know that name?"

"No. Who is he?"

"You mean, who was he? He was killed in a shoot-out with a rival group about a year and a half ago. It was a pretty big story because he was something of a mysterious figure in the militia world."

"Okay. What about Charkin's finances?"

"Not exactly a model of consistency. He spent most of the year broke, broken up by intermittent cash infusions. Usually at five thousand a clip; there were nine of them."

"That figures." My assumption is that he hadn't had a chance to deposit the last five thousand before he was killed.

"One interesting thing. He wrote a five-thousand-dollar check to Tina Welker."

That's all Sam has for me, but it certainly gives me plenty to think about after the Nichols meeting.

Laurie is dressed and ready by the time Nichols arrives. She looks fresh and clean, like she just got out of the shower. When I get out of the shower, I look like I need a shower. I don't know why that is, but it's another mystery I hope to have time to focus on when I retire.

Nichols calls when he's downstairs, so I go down to the lobby to meet him and bring up more coffee and muffins for all of us. These are some seriously good muffins.

When we get to the room, I introduce Nichols and tell him

that Laurie will be sitting in on our meeting. I add that she is my investigator and a former cop.

"I thought we might meet alone," Nichols says.

"I trust this woman with my life, Senator. To ask her to leave would be an insult." It's a takeoff of a line from Michael Corleone in *Godfather II,* but I don't think Nichols gets it.

In any event, he smiles and says to Laurie, "Agent Spodek told me about you. She said that you were the one that wasn't a pain in the ass."

Cindy Spodek is the friend of ours at the FBI who set up my initial meeting with Nichols. "That Agent Spodek is quite a kidder," I say. "To what do we owe this visit?"

I'm hoping he's here to provide me with more information about Jerry Donnelly; my first choice would be for him to tell me that Donnelly has confessed to the murders and that Matt Jantzen is being released from jail even as we speak.

That's not it. "It's about your investigation into Peter Charkin."

That's almost as good. "What about it?"

"You spoke to Daniel McCaskill."

I nod. "I already knew that; I'm the one that spoke to him. How did you know?"

"I'm an FBI agent; I know things. Keep that in mind."

"I'll commit it to memory." Then, "Is that all you have for me?"

"I'm here to receive information, not to dispense it."

"Then you drove a long way for nothing. You should take a couple of muffins home with you, so it's not a total loss."

Laurie rolls her eyes, a sure sign that I am being obnoxious. Laurie rolls her eyes a lot.

"Let's go through the motions anyway," Nichols says. "Can I assume you spoke to him as part of your investigation into Charkin's death?"

"You can."

"Can you be more specific?"

"Maybe. If you tell me why you want to know."

"The Bureau has an active investigation ongoing into the militia group of which McCaskill is a member."

Laurie says, "And Charkin was a member as well?"

Nichols nods. "He was." He turns back to me. "The Bureau has two, noncompeting interests here. First, we want to know if you have relevant information that can help us. And second, we do not want you to do anything that would constitute interference in our efforts."

"Understood," I say. "I have two noncompeting interests as well. First, I want to defend my client as best I can. And second, I want to defend my client as best I can."

"We should each be able to accomplish our goals," Nichols says.

"Good. So let's set up ground rules. We tell each other any relevant information we have or acquire, as long as it doesn't go against our respective interests."

"Fair enough."

Laurie pretends to dab at a tear. "This is a beautiful moment." It's the kind of sarcastic comment I would make, and I would roll my eyes at her, if I knew how. My experience in this area is as an eye-rollee, not an eye-roller.

"You go first."

"We have reason to believe that the militia group of which Charkin was a member is planning a significant event. I really have little information beyond that and couldn't share it if I did. But we have no reason to believe that Charkin, who obviously died two years ago, was a part of it."

"But Charkin was a member?"

Nichols nods. "On the fringe. Not a serious player, and certainly not part of leadership."

"Might he have gotten money from them? Five thousand dollars in cash was found in his apartment."

"Anything is possible, but I am at a loss as to why they would have paid him anything. I believe it's your turn."

"I'm afraid I have nothing for you right now. I learned in the discovery documents that the police had McCaskill on their suspect list originally, before the DNA ruled him out. It also said that he was a militia member. So I went to talk to him about it, to get a sense of whether he was a viable candidate to have killed Charkin and Tina Welker."

"And his response?"

"He found me to be irritating and obnoxious and threatened to forcibly evict me from his house. Go figure."

"Anything else?" Nichols asks, probably frustrated at how little I have to offer.

"Maybe. I have reason to believe that soon after I left, McCaskill placed a call to a guy named Gavin Helms."

"You're tapping McCaskill's phone?" Nichols asks, barely concealing his incredulity.

"No chance. That would be illegal; as an FBI agent you should know that. Think of this as a very strong hunch that you can take to the bank. I am great at hunches."

"But you're sure that McCaskill called him?"

"Positive." My assumption is that the FBI might be monitoring McCaskill's phone, since they seem so interested in him. They would have no way of knowing about his burner phone, though; we only know about it because Charlie Tilton was resourceful enough to steal its wrapping from off McCaskill's couch.

"Do you know where Helms is?" Nichols asks.

"No."

"Are McCaskill, and the people he works with, capable of murder?" Laurie asks.

Nichols doesn't hesitate. "Absolutely."

Neither of us has said anything of value, but we both say that we will abide by our agreement to share information when possible. If it doesn't benefit my client, I will undoubtedly renege on that agreement.

Even though I was hoping for better, I think Nichols was being straight with me, so I give him a muffin to take back with him.

Never let it be said that Andy Carpenter isn't gracious.

The meeting with Nichols was disappointing.

When I found out he wanted to talk, I had this hope, admittedly a long shot but still a hope, that he would have incriminating information about Jerry Donnelly.

But he obviously didn't; instead he had his own militia-related agenda. The militia side of it is interesting to me in that it demonstrated that Charkin was involved with people who are known to be violent. I might even try to put it before a jury.

But at the end of the day it doesn't fit into any theory I can come up with, at least based on my current knowledge. Charkin was likely on the Liberator payroll; that is probably where the cash infusions came from. His brother assumed that as well. Charkin was performing a service for them, and I'd like to know what it was, but I just don't know why they would kill him.

Donnelly is a different story because of the drug connection. By all accounts Donnelly is also a violent guy, capable of murder. Charkin could easily have been into him for money; for a period he was desperate enough to scam his own brother for some.

But what makes Donnelly's involvement especially likely is Stokan's going after me. Donnelly doesn't know me, and generally it's only people who know me that dislike me. His only interest in my investigation must be a concern for what I could uncover.

He, or his people, wouldn't have sent Stokan after me unless they were worried about what I might find out. Since the only thing I am looking into is the double murder, it's a logical conclusion that he has some culpability.

One puzzling thing to come out of Sam's report is the $5,000 check that Charkin wrote to Tina Welker. I can think of two possible reasons for it. One is that she needed money; her mother was ill and the family may have been strapped.

Charkin was at that moment relatively rich, by his standards, because of the cash he had been accumulating. So maybe he was just a generous guy who cared about Tina and gave her the money. Maybe it was a loan, to be repaid with interest. No way to know.

Another possibility is that he was using her to hide the money for some reason that isn't yet apparent. That makes less sense because he wrote her a check; if he dealt in cash so much, one would think that he would have given her cash and told her to hide it. Writing a check to her is not an effective way to conceal anything.

I might as well follow up on that because I have nothing else to do. So I head back to Augusta General Hospital and Medical Center to talk to Ginny Lawson again. Ginny was Tina's friend and coworker and was forthcoming last time.

I call ahead, but she is in with a patient. I leave a message that I'm on the way; hopefully she'll be able to see me.

When I arrive, I tell the receptionist that I'm here, an unnecessary act because Ginny sees me through a glass door and comes out. She smiles and invites me into the back.

On the way, I almost bang into a woman pushing a cart. Bags of dark red liquid are hanging above the cart. When the woman moves on, I say to Ginny, "Is that what I think it was?"

"Sure was. Blood make you squeamish?"

"It's on the list of things that do, yes. What is she doing with it?"

"Taking it to be irradiated. Makes it okay to give to patients whose immune systems have been taken down."

"Oh."

We go to an examining room. "Making any progress?" she asks.

"Less than I'd like. You told me last time that Tina was having money problems?"

"Oh, yes. Plenty. They never had much money anyway, but her father left her mother, and then her mother got sick. Tina was the only one bringing in any money, and believe me, working here doesn't make you rich."

"Would she have borrowed from friends?"

"Maybe. She never asked me, but she would know I didn't have any myself."

"Peter Charkin gave her five thousand dollars."

Ginny does a double take. "Wow. I'm surprised."

"Why?"

"Taking that money sort of implies a commitment; you don't do that with someone you're going to break up with twenty minutes later. I didn't think they were that serious. But I guess if she was desperate enough . . ."

"Did you ever spend time with Charkin? With or without Tina?"

"A couple of times, but Tina was certainly there."

I take out my photos of Stokan and McCaskill. "Did you ever see either of them?"

Ginny takes the time to carefully look at them. "I don't think so, and I'm very good at remembering faces."

I thank Ginny and tell her that I'll try not to bother her again.

"No bother. Just call if you need me, but I'm going to be pretty busy. It's going to be chaos here; they're going to be working on the machines on Saturday. Probably easier to reach me at home."

I thank her and leave, being careful on the way out to avoid people pushing carts.

found more than I expected, but probably less than we need," Charlie Tilton says.

We're in his office about to discuss his efforts to find flaws in the prosecution's DNA evidence. It was and remains by far the most significant factor; if not for that, Matt Jantzen would never have been suspected or charged and could certainly not be convicted.

"I'll take that as a positive development. Let's hear it."

He hands me a folder. "You're better off reading it; a lot of it is technical crap that would put us both to sleep."

"Summarize it."

"There are some chain-of-custody issues, mostly time lapses. Some potential mislabeling, trace presence of EDTA, and examples of problems the agency has had on past cases. It will definitely give you something to talk about in court."

"You find an expert who will testify to it?"

"I did. Professor of criminology at Boston University. You want to talk to her?"

"Not yet. Let me go through this first. Then we can bring her in closer to trial."

"We're not that far from trial now."

"Don't remind me." I hold up the folder. "Why did you say this is less than we need?"

"Because at the end of the day it's all bullshit. Jantzen's blood was at the scene, on the victim's hands, and none of this explains that away. You and I know it, and so will the jury, no matter what you say."

"I'm planning to say it with an appealing smile."

"You might want to work on that; I saw you in action with McCaskill. You didn't seem like a charm school graduate."

"Ye of little faith."

"So what have you been up to? You need to keep me up-to-date. If Henry Stokan succeeds in killing you, I'll have to pick up the ball."

"That is not likely to happen."

"Why not?"

"Mr. Stokan got a taste of how tough I can be . . . when I'm standing behind Marcus Clark."

"What happened?"

I tell him about the incident with Stokan and his friend in the park, and how he later implicated Donnelly in sending him after me.

"He gave up Donnelly's name?" Charlie asks, obviously surprised.

"He did. When you meet Marcus, you'll understand."

"I'm glad I didn't write Stokan's life insurance policy."

"Is he dumb enough to tell Donnelly what happened?"

"Maybe, but probably not. Though Donnelly has ways of finding out details. You said that Stokan had a friend with him?"

"Yes, but he spent most of my time with him unconscious, so we didn't get to chat much."

"That's one way Donnelly could find out. The friend could tell him as a way to curry favor. Risky, but the guy is probably not that bright in the first place. You still have Marcus following him?"

I shake my head. "No, Marcus is working his way up the chain of command. Right now he's in the process of locating Lyle Carmody."

"Name does not ring a bell," Tilton says.

"He's one of Donnelly's people, in charge of, among other things, dealing drugs in this area."

"Stokan fingered him as well?"

I shrug. "Marcus is Marcus."

"What are you going to do when you find Carmody?"

"Don't know yet; but we need to rattle some cages. Got any ideas?"

He nods. "Yeah, have Jantzen plead guilty so you can go back to New York."

"New Jersey."

"Whatever. You are treading in dangerous territory. Be careful."

His warning is sincere, so I promise that I will be careful. The problem is that being careful often doesn't do the trick for me; I wind up in dangerous situations anyway.

I leave to head back to the hotel. The plan is to walk the dogs and then Laurie and I will go to dinner. Dinners take place early here; Damariscotta heads toward ghost town status every evening by nine o'clock.

When I walk in, Laurie is standing about six feet from the television, watching it. Her body language and facial expression indicates to me that she is not watching *Seinfeld* or *Modern Family*.

"Have you seen this?" She points at the television.

I don't answer, but I walk over and look. A local reporter is standing in front of a river, talking into a microphone. Instead of listening to him, I turn to Laurie. "What's going on?"

"They fished Henry Stokan's body out of the river about an hour ago."

I let that sink in. "Charlie Tilton knows what he's talking about."

I may be getting self-centered in my old age. But the truth is that I think Stokan was murdered for the purpose of sending me a message. Just like Stokan's following me in the first place was Donnelly's way of getting me to back off, I think this killing had the same purpose.

That's obviously not the only reason, and not even the most likely one. Donnelly might have found out, possibly through the other idiot, as Charlie Tilton suggested might happen, that Stokan gave up his name to Marcus. The other idiot's body has not been found, so maybe Donnelly is rewarding him, or at least letting him off the hook.

I know I'm an extraordinarily scary guy, but for the life of me I don't know what Donnelly is afraid of. I am not close to exposing anything meaningful about his operation, and even if I was, so what?

The worst that could happen, from Donnelly's point of view, is that I could find out he was supplying drugs to Charkin. He'd swat that problem away like a fly, especially since there were buffers, like Carmody, between him and the actual dealing.

Yet he's been reacting all along to me in a way that seems wildly disproportionate to the threat. And getting rid of Stokan was an example of literal overkill.

But clearly something was going on with Charkin, something serious. I thought all along that a double murder as retribution for failing to pay a drug debt seemed unlikely, and I'm even more sure of that now.

Charkin was involved with something heavy, something that was important to Donnelly and his operation. When I know what that was, I'll know everything. Until then, I know nothing.

Carmody is obviously the next place for us to probe, but I've decided to take a different approach. We could confront him head-on, in which case Marcus could probably coerce him into giving up Donnelly. That wouldn't get us anywhere and would probably buy Carmody the same fate as Stokan's.

I guess we could eliminate Donnelly's whole organization like that, one at a time. Marcus could intimidate everyone working for Donnelly into ratting him out, then Donnelly could kill the poor guys.

The idea has a unique appeal and some poetic justice to it, but it would take too long and not help my client. So we're not doing it that way; instead, Marcus is going to track Carmody's movements in case it leads us to anything meaningful.

Sam Willis provided Marcus with Carmody's home address, the kind of car he drives, and his license plate number. Sam is also monitoring Carmody's phone to see if he makes any calls we can determine are significant.

Tonight I am just going to have take-out dinner with Laurie, take the dogs for a walk, and settle in to read the discovery documents again. Steinkamp has added to the pile with more information, which, while suggestive, does not implicate Matt any further.

I'm also going to go over the DNA information that Charlie Tilton has prepared. If we are successful in challenging that, victory will be ours. Unfortunately, even he has indicated that the "smoking DNA gun" is not to be found.

At around nine o'clock I'm in what passes for a den when I hear a knock on the door. Laurie answers it and I see that Marcus has come by. Since he's staying in the room next to ours, I guess he figured this was just as easy as calling.

I don't know what he wants, and since I wouldn't be able to understand him anyway, I let Laurie deal with him. I'm sure I'll get the translated version if it's important.

"Andy, can you come in here?" Laurie calls, so I put down the folder I'm going through and head that way.

"What's going on? Hey, Marcus, didn't realize you were here," I lie.

"Marcus has been following our friend Mr. Carmody. He's been watching him deliver goods to customers and make collections. But tonight, right after dark, he met with someone in a deserted parking lot behind a business. Nothing was exchanged; all they did was talk. Here's the photograph he took."

My first thought, before I focus on what is in the photo, is that Marcus has some kind of night camera, or infrared lens, or something. My second thought is that I probably paid for it.

My third thought is more significant, because I've now seen the photo of the two men. "Was this taken behind the Maine Lighthouse brewery?"

"How did you know?" Laurie sounds surprised.

"Because I know that guy. He's Mike Mitchell, owner of the brewery, and friend of Peter Charkin. And I have a hunch they're not comparing craft beers."

After Marcus leaves, Laurie and I stay up until midnight discussing our next steps, before going to bed.

It's a sign that we're getting to be an old married couple; we used to be able to discuss murder and drugs until at least two o'clock in the morning.

The day I went to see him, Mike Mitchell obviously lied to me about everything except how to make beer. And maybe he even lied about that. At this point, if he told me he had a barrel full of barley, I'd be willing to bet it was hops.

He said he had no idea where Peter Charkin was getting his drugs, and although Stokan denied it, it had to be through Carmody. I asked Mitchell point-blank if he had ever heard of Donnelly or Stokan, and he said that he hadn't.

Charkin's optometrist brother had told me that Mitchell and Peter Charkin were friends. I think he believed that because he wouldn't have a reason to lie. But just in case, I'm glad I didn't let him do laser surgery on me.

But Mitchell was clearly lying when I spoke to him, which leaves us with the two questions standard in cases like this. Why was he lying, and what should we do about it?

My answers, when I started tonight's conversation with Laurie, were "I have no idea" and "Beats the hell out of me." By the time we're finished with our talk, my two answers are "I have no idea" and "Confront the son of a bitch."

I call Sam Willis at midnight. I don't apologize for calling so late because he answers "Talk to me" on the first ring in a voice that is obviously wide awake. Sam definitely has a weird side.

"I need an address for Mike, or Michael, Mitchell. He lives up here and owns the Maine Lighthouse brewery."

"You want the home address?"

"Yes."

"Anything else?"

"Not right now."

"I'll call you back."

I hang up, put the discovery documents back in their folder, and head for the bedroom. On the way, the phone rings. It's Sam with the address. As a computer guy, he is worth his weight in gigabytes.

I give him another assignment: to monitor Mitchell's phone calls tomorrow. Then I thank him and hang up.

At six twenty in the morning Laurie and I leave the hotel to head for Mitchell's house in Bristol. I'm not happy about this because the muffins don't make their appearance until six forty-five. But in the legal business, you do what you have to do.

We're in place in front of Mitchell's house at seven. A car is in the driveway, but that doesn't necessarily mean he's home. If he's a morning guy, he might be at work already, which would mean I missed the muffins for nothing.

Laurie insisted on coming along, even though I told her I'd be safe at seven in the morning in a nice neighborhood talking to a guy who makes beer for a living. She was unconvinced, which is why she is sitting in the passenger seat.

Since the purpose is to surprise Mitchell, we've decided to do so at a time and place he would not expect. It might be jarring enough to get him to make a mistake. Certainly had I called and requested a meeting in his office, he would have had a chance to prepare for all possibilities.

After twenty minutes, the front door opens and Mitchell comes out. I get out of the car as Laurie waits behind, watching in case I need help.

"Mike! Mike Mitchell!" I yell as I walk toward him. "What the hell are the odds of running into you here?"

He looks bewildered as he places my face and that I'm standing in front of his house at this hour, or any hour. "Mr. Carpenter. You know where I live?"

"I'm a professional investigator; stuff like that comes easy to me."

"You could have called my office."

"I'm aware of that, but I was really anxious to know why you lied to me, so I didn't want to wait."

A flash of worry crosses his face. "Lied to you? Don't be ridiculous."

"You told me you didn't know where Peter Charkin got his drugs, and that you never heard of Jerry Donnelly."

"Both of those things are true."

"Really? Lyle Carmody didn't mention anything about it last night?"

Mitchell takes a few moments to digest my words. "It's not what you think."

"Enlighten me."

"Peter was an addict; you know that already. He was into Donnelly and Carmody for some serious money and had no way to pay them back. I went to them and said that I'd cover it, over time. That time ended last night; I met Carmody and gave him the last payment."

I'm pretty sure he's lying, though he's damn good at it. Marcus said that nothing changed hands last night. It was dark so possibly he is wrong, but Marcus is rarely wrong.

"Why did they kill Charkin and Tina Welker?"

"That's crazy; they had no reason to. I was paying the debt. I could have stopped when Peter died, but I didn't. I wanted them out of my life for good."

"Why did they kill Stokan?"

"I don't know anything about that. Look, these are dangerous people. I don't know what they do or how they operate, and I don't want to. I said I would cover Peter's debt, and I did. I want this over, and until you just showed up, I thought it was."

"What about Danny McCaskill and his buddy Gavin Helms? McCaskill had some interesting things to say to me."

I'm lying about that and taking a stab in the dark. If Charkin was involved with McCaskill, then Mitchell might have been as well. I'm just looking to see if I get a reaction.

I don't. Mitchell just looks confused. "Who the hell are they?"

It was worth a shot, and no harm was done. "We'll talk again soon."

He shakes his head. "I don't think we will."

My conversation with Mitchell essentially left me back where I started.

Once again I'm almost certain he's still lying, but it leaves me with the same two questions that I've yet to answer: Why is he lying? And what should we do about it?

Though he displayed coolness under pressure when I confronted him, his story simply does not hold up. For one thing, it is highly unlikely he would have paid Peter Charkin's drug debt. They were friends, not brothers.

And if he did pay it, he would not have done it directly. He would not have wanted to be involved with those people; he would have given the money to Charkin to take it to them. And lastly, he would not have continued paying after Charkin died. No one is that good a friend.

Even if all of that didn't make it obvious to me that he was lying, his meeting with Carmody last night was the clincher. He was not making a final payment; Marcus said that nothing changed hands.

So why would they have had to meet? If their entire relationship was about Mitchell paying Charkin's drug debt, why sneak off like that to talk? Were they exchanging verbal recipes?

I'd like to learn more about Charkin's real-life relationship with Mitchell, not the fantasy one that Mitchell presented. To that end I call Charkin's brother, Robert. I'm hoping to reach him before he spends the day asking patients which lenses help them see better.

He does come to the phone, and I ask, "You told me that Mitchell kept your brother on at the brewery longer than he should have out of friendship."

"That's what Mitchell told me, yes."

"How close were they?"

Robert pauses to think about it. "To be honest, I hadn't thought very close at all, but when Mitchell told me that, I had no reason to doubt it."

"If I asked you if Mitchell would pay for your brother's drug debts, would you think it was possible?"

"Anything's possible, but I can't imagine that was the case. Is that what you think was going on?"

"I'm just throwing theories against the wall. Here's another one. Could Mitchell have been supplying your brother with drugs?"

"I really doubt that also. If he was giving him the drugs, why would he fire him for taking them?"

"Good point. Let's try scenario number three. Could they have been in business together?"

Robert pauses before answering. "The drug business? I have no knowledge of that, but of the three scenarios you presented, that's the most likely. Peter would have been a part of anything that could make him money; that's just the way he was."

I thank Robert and end the call. Laurie has scheduled some interviews with friends and coworkers of Tina Welker's, so I drop her off at the hotel and head for Charlie Tilton's office. I've found him to be smart and a good sounding board, so I want to tell him what's gone on, and maybe together we can come up with a plan.

When I get to Charlie's office, he pours some coffee and we sit down so I can fill him in. "Who did you piss off now? Al Capone?"

"He's dead," I say. "Try and keep up."

"Speaking of dead, I have to ask this question, even though I don't really want to know the answer. Did your friend Marcus put Stokan in the river?"

"No. I suspect that was your friend Donnelly who did that."

I go on to tell him about Mitchell meeting with Carmody last night, and our conversation in front of his house this morning.

"Wow," Charlie says when I'm finished. "Around here when we lawyers want to interview a witness, we set up a deposition, hire a stenographer; it's a big production. I didn't realize you can just accost the person in their driveway."

"You have much to learn from me. So what do you think?"

"I think our friend Mr. Mitchell is lying through his beer-brewing teeth."

"Right you are. Any idea as to why he might be doing that?"

"Maybe Mitchell and Peter Charkin shared a habit, and in Mitchell's case it's ongoing? It's not something he'd want public."

"That's the easiest explanation, and it's certainly possible. But it feels like there's something more here. Don't forget, Stokan told Marcus that Carmody and Donnelly were not Charkin's suppliers."

"Maybe he lied."

"Could be. But if he was going to withhold something, which is not easy to do when Marcus is involved, he would have held back Donnelly's name. That was the dangerous reveal, which is demonstrated by Stokan making that unscheduled appearance in the river."

"And then there's the five grand," Charlie says.

"Right. Money was coming to Charkin . . . cash money. That

doesn't usually happen to a guy with no job, no apparent source of income, and a drug habit."

"Could have been that militia thing with McCaskill."

I shake my head. "I don't think so, although the visit from FBI agent Nichols has been bugging me."

"Why?"

"It was overkill. First of all, just him knowing that we spoke to McCaskill must mean that McCaskill is under surveillance. All I did was talk to him. If Nichols drives all the way up here to meet with everyone McCaskill talks to, he'd better hope McCaskill doesn't have much of a social life, or he'll be on the road twenty-four/seven."

Charlie nods. "And Nichols would have no reason to think you're talking to him about anything the FBI should be interested in. And in fact you weren't."

"Right. Something heavy must be going down . . . something the Bureau is really worried about. They're covering all their bases."

"Let's get back to Charkin. Donnelly obviously needed him for something, though I have no idea what. But then why kill him?"

"I suspect Donnelly is the type who needs someone until he doesn't need them anymore."

Charlie nods. "And not to make matters worse, but none of this gets our client off the hook."

"I'm hoping we can point to other bad guys and say, 'Look, they might have done it.'" Then, "Of course, we'll need to find bad guys that bleed Jantzen's blood."

"That could be a problem, even for a hotshot New York lawyer."

"New Jersey."

"Whatever."

have to approach situations like this with two different mindsets.

So I bring both mindsets with me when I take the three dogs for a walk this evening.

On the one hand I am trying to figure out what the hell is going on. I want to know all the facts, what every one of the players has done and why they have done it.

On the other hand, I have to think about what I can present to the jury, and how I can persuade them. The two sets of facts are not identical. Some evidence may not be admissible, and some, even though I believe it to be true, may not neatly fit into my case strategy.

So I head down both tracks at the same time and hope that they blend together. Sometimes they do and sometimes they don't.

Right now I believe that the murderer came from the lawless firm of Donnelly, Carmody, and Stokan. But I have no way to get the jury to believe it, even if I can get evidence of their involvement with Charkin admitted in court.

Not only do I not have anything concrete to tie them to Tina Welker's house that night, but I don't have logic on my side.

Not only won't the jury buy it, but the lack of that logic makes it hard for me to accept it myself.

I don't know why they would have wanted to kill Charkin, but that's not my only problem. The way they did it makes no sense.

Why a home invasion? And why an elaborate frame of someone they didn't even know, namely Matt Jantzen? If Donnelly wanted Charkin dead, why not just kill him and dump his body in the river, like he did with Stokan? Or why not bury the body where it could never be found?

To set it up as a home invasion, killing an innocent bystander in the process, just doesn't ring true. I've dealt with enough people like Donnelly to know that it's not how they operate. He didn't have to frame Matt; Donnelly wasn't going to get nailed for Charkin's murder.

The trial is bearing down, and I have more questions than answers.

That's because I don't have any answers.

Right as I walk back into our suite with the dogs, Sam calls to report on his phone reconnaissance. He's continued to monitor McCaskill's calls, though nothing interesting has come up. McCaskill has stopped making calls of any consequence, not even to Gavin Helms's burner phone. I don't know if that is of great significance; Helms is part of the leadership of the Liberators, and McCaskill may be just a bit player.

"Sam, can you use the GPS information on Helms's phone to find out where he is?" I'm asking because it might be a bargaining chip I can use with the FBI; Nichols had asked me if I knew Helms's whereabouts.

"You got it."

"What about Mitchell? Anything to report on his calls?"

"That's a little tougher. I'm covering his cell phone; he doesn't have a landline at home. But he's got a brewery business with a lot of employees. It's impossible to track all the calls made from there, and even if we could, there would be no way to know who within the building is actually making them."

"I understand. Anything interesting on his cell phone calls?"

"Just one thing. He's also made two calls to a burner phone. No way to know whose it is, but it seems suspicious."

"I agree. Can you also track that phone's location using GPS?" Sam has shown an ability to track the location of cell phones through the phone company computers. Cell phones have GPS devices built into them; it has become a valuable tool for police, as well as the famed Andy Carpenter defense team.

"Maybe. I'll have to check it out. Not all burners have GPS systems in them. Same thing is true with Helms's phone. Sorry, I should have checked all of this already."

"Not your fault. Thanks, Sam, please keep me posted."

Laurie has overheard all of this, and when I get off the phone, she hands me a glass of wine. "Let's sit down; I want to talk to you about something."

"Uh-oh." I sit next to her on the couch. "Okay, I'm ready."

"I think we should get Corey up here." She's talking about Corey Douglas, who partners with Laurie and Marcus in the K Team investigative firm.

"Why?"

"You're going to be in trial, so we'll be shorthanded in the field. We also need to make something happen; maybe Corey's presence can help."

"Let me think about it," I say, probably surprising her. I'm sure she thought I was going to reject it out of hand, hence the wine.

"How long will it take you to think?"

"Not sure."

The doorbell rings and I go to answer it. When I open it, Corey Douglas is standing there with Simon Garfunkel, his partner and former police dog.

I turn back to Laurie. "I guess I'm finished thinking."

She smiles. "I didn't think it was something that could wait, and I knew you would come around."

Corey comes into the room. "Thanks for getting the room. A suite really wasn't necessary."

I turn to Laurie again. She shrugs. "We travel in style."

Simon runs into the room because he sees his buddy Tara. Hunter jumps up to greet the newcomer as well, since he is devoted to Tara and will emulate whatever she does. I think Tara's mothering him as well; the other night they slept next to each other, with Tara's paw draped over him.

Sebastian doesn't think Simon's arrival is significant enough to disturb his rest; Sebastian chooses to emulate an anvil.

Corey says that Simon needs a walk, so we all decide to go. Tara and Simon are typically eager for the adventure. Sebastian acts as if he'd rather be waterboarded, so we let him sit this one out.

Three dogs and three humans; we make quite a caravan. Along the way Laurie and I update Corey on all that has gone on. He's familiar with a lot of it; he's been talking to Laurie from New Jersey.

Once we're back, he asks, "Okay, where do you want me tomorrow?"

"I think it's best you start by putting Mitchell under surveillance. Maybe he'll make a mistake or do something revealing."

"You mean like writing out a confession to the murders and leaving it on the street?"

"That would be nice."

The burner phone that Mike Mitchell has been calling belongs to Jerry Donnelly.

Actually, it's been more than one phone; Donnelly apparently switches his out fairly often. But the good news is that he uses high-class burners, which come with GPS trackers.

Sam isolated the GPS signal to a house in a gated community in Freeport. Marcus set up camp there and, after a number of days, finally saw Donnelly leaving to go into town to a restaurant. Apparently, he doesn't get out much.

Sam tracked the movement of the phone to that restaurant, and Marcus surreptitiously snapped a photo, so we are positive it was Donnelly who was carrying it.

That feels like a step forward, but really isn't. Clearly Mitchell is dirty. Between his meeting with Carmody and his calling Donnelly, there's no question about that. But Mitchell's having business with the two of them does absolutely nothing to tie either of them to Charkin's murder.

Marcus wants to confront Donnelly but is the only one who thinks it's a good idea. Marcus wants to confront everybody and has full confidence he can induce the person he confronts to provide whatever information we are looking for.

It's just too big a risk, with not enough potential for reward.

Donnelly, like anyone in his position, would be well protected. Even if we were able to penetrate it, and I believe Marcus could do just that, Donnelly's not about to confess to murder. And even if he did, it would be inadmissible because it would have been made under duress.

Marcus specializes in duress.

I can't remember the last trial I have headed into with less ammunition. I can possibly tie Charkin to dangerous people like Carmody on the drug side and maybe McCaskill on the militia side, but I can't come close to implicating them in the murders of Charkin and Tina Welker.

Things might become clearer and open up avenues of investigation if I could figure out why the killer wanted Charkin dead. He seems like a bit player, sort of a pathetic figure, and it's hard to fathom how he could have been such a major danger to Donnelly.

I'm downstairs having a muffin and coffee and preparing to head to court when Corey comes in. He's been watching Mitchell for five days, without having reported anything unusual going on. "You got a minute?"

I nod. "But not much more. Apparently they start court on time around here."

"I was going to call you last night, but it was late. There's a truck that has arrived at Mitchell's brewery; it came two of the last three days. I don't know if it's making a delivery or a pickup, because it goes into the indoor loading dock. The outside of the truck says CASTLE FARM PRODUCTS, INC."

"Why are we interested in it?"

"Two reasons. One, it shows up after closing time, about thirty minutes after what I assume is when the day shift leaves. I thought that was unusual, so I had Sam check out Castle Farm Products. That brings me to my second reason; there's no company named Castle Farm Products. According to Sam, it doesn't exist."

"Interesting," I say, understating the case.

"Here's another tidbit for you. The license plate is a fake; Sam says it was never issued by the state. I didn't ask Sam how he knows that because I didn't want to hear the answer."

"I know the feeling. What do you think we should do with this information?"

"I think I should wait for the next time the truck shows up and follow it. Maybe that will tell us something, and maybe it won't. But it can't hurt to know."

"Good idea. I wish I could go with you."

"I can handle it."

"I know; I would just like to come up with a way to get out of going to court."

Corey gets up and walks away, but then seems to remember something and comes back. "By the way, did Laurie mention that Sam is on the way up here?"

"No."

"He'll be here this afternoon; we need him for some electronic surveillance work."

"So I need to get him a room?"

Corey shakes his head. "No, Laurie already reserved him a suite."

"Maybe we should just make an offer to buy the hotel."

Corey shrugs. "Your call. It's a nice place." He picks up a muffin. "And great muffins."

Jury selection is different on Planet Maine than it is back on Earth.

The procedures are basically the same. The lawyers get to question the potential jurors in voir dire, we have challenges we can use to dismiss them preemptively and for cause, and we're looking to seat twelve people and three alternates.

The difference is that the prospective jury pool is made up of Mainers, rather than earthlings. It is immediately detectable in their attitude; they actually want to be here.

I am overgeneralizing, but people back home view getting summoned to jury duty as a stroke of bad luck; they say of their neighbor, "How come he doesn't get called?" The people here seem to think they are performing a community service, that they are stepping up to fulfill a worthy obligation.

And they are nice. Actually, that's not the right word; some of the people back home are nice as well. Here they are earnest; they want to help, and they strive to keep an open mind.

Before we started asking them questions verbally, they filled out a questionnaire, mostly biographical details. They did it in a room of about seventy people.

In a situation like this back home, everybody is talking and grumbling during the process. Here there was dead silence in the room, as people pored over the questionnaire and filled it out with great care. The atmosphere was such that you would think they were taking the SAT.

Charlie surprised me by showing up today; his work was all supposed to be behind-the-scenes. "I wanted to watch a hotshot New York lawyer in action."

I corrected him by saying, "New Jersey."

"Whatever."

There are two types of Mainers: those who work with their hands and those who hire people who work with their hands. This is generally true in New Jersey as well, but there the lines are not drawn quite so vividly, or quite so geographically.

When it comes to challenging and accepting jurors, I do what I do back home; I go with my gut. Obviously there are some triggers; if a person has been victimized by a home invasion or is one of ten siblings, the other nine of whom are police officers, I don't want them on the jury.

On the other side, if a person says that he practices a religion that doesn't believe in DNA, that's an automatic keeper. So far we haven't run into anyone like that.

Charlie is helpful during the process. He's smart and understands the sensibilities of these people; he also either knows or has information on some of them.

But basically, if the potential juror seems like a normal, reasonably intelligent person, I just take my best guess. Since all of these people seem normal and reasonably intelligent, we are finished selecting a jury of five men and seven women in just over a day and a half.

Matt has been quiet through most of it. It can be fairly stunning to realize that everybody is gathered to decide whether you will spend the rest of your life in freedom or behind bars. If he has an opinion on any particular juror, he doesn't voice it. That's just as well, since I wouldn't listen to it anyway.

As always, it's a simultaneously boring and frustrating process. It's boring because it's, well, boring. Earnest people who are trying to please don't often say fascinating stuff.

It's frustrating because there is no way to keep score. We don't know whether we are doing well, and we won't know until they come in with their verdict.

When we're done, Matt asks, "How do you think we did?"

"Beats the hell out of me," I say.

This causes Matt to turn and ask Charlie the same question. He responds, "I agree with Andy."

Matt shrugs. "I guess that's it then."

I am just about to tell Matt to have a nice weekend, then I realize how ridiculous that is. I'd also like to tell him that next week could bring good news, but the truth is that it will consist of Steinkamp presenting his case for Matt being convicted of a double murder.

"See you Monday" is all I can come up with.

There have been some developments regarding the truck that's been showing up at Maine Lighthouse brewery," Laurie says.

I've just gotten back from walking the dogs, only to find that Laurie, Corey, Sam, and Marcus are all in our room, apparently waiting for me.

"Is that the purpose of this meeting?"

"Yes. A lot has gone on while you've been off having fun in court."

"I'm all ears." The truth is that I haven't been focusing on the truck or Maine Lighthouse brewery much at all. For one thing, I've been busy on trial preparation; for another, it just feels like there is a huge chasm between that truck and anything having to do with the murders.

I haven't asked for an update and I haven't received one, though that is clearly about to change.

Laurie turns the floor over to Corey. "As you know, the truck has a fake company name on it; there is no such business as Castle Farm Products. It originates in Canada, arrives at Maine Lighthouse brewery after hours, and drops off its cargo. It leaves empty."

"How do you know that?"

"We followed it for two hours. After that, physical surveillance was no longer necessary."

"Why not?"

"The driver stopped at a rest area. We used the opportunity to incorporate electronic devices. Sam?"

"There's a GPS device on the truck itself and a camera and microphone in the interior."

"You got into the truck?"

"Yes, it only took a couple of minutes. Corey made sure that the driver did not come back prematurely."

Corey shrugs. "Intervention wasn't required. The guy sat down and had a meal in the food court."

"And are they liable to detect the surveillance equipment?"

Sam looks wounded. "Andy . . ."

"Okay. So where does that leave us?"

"The next time the truck comes down, we'll know about it. We'll also be able to watch it being loaded and unloaded."

"What are we expecting to learn?" I ask, though I know where they are going with this.

"What they are bringing in," Laurie says. "It is our considered opinion that it has nothing to do with beer. Canada is not a source of hops and barley; some if it is grown here in Maine, but most in the Western states. And other trucks have been seen making deliveries of those products during business hours."

"Drugs?" I ask.

"That is our best guess," she says.

"They just drive it across the border?"

She nods. "Apparently, but that is still to be determined."

"And why do they bring it to the brewery? Just for storage?"

"Still to be determined, but that seems likely. Trucks go in and out of there all the time, so the ones carrying illegal contraband can go unnoticed. It makes sense for Donnelly."

I think they might well be right, and I will be pleased if we somehow get to reveal it and the cops can use it to put Mitchell, and maybe Donnelly, away for a long time. But my focus has to be on how that can help me in trial.

In a best case, I'll be able to use it to tell the jury a story. It will take some imagination, but maybe I'll say that Peter Charkin, working for Mitchell at the brewery, found out what was going on.

I'd go on to say that Charkin used the information to try to blackmail Mitchell, but didn't realize that he was also blackmailing Donnelly. Donnelly didn't take kindly to it and killed Charkin. Tina Welker had the bad luck to be with Charkin at the time, so she was killed also, in a way that made it look like a home invasion.

In a second-best case, and that's pretty much the most I can ever hope for, I'll be able to point out that Charkin was involved with some bad people, people who would not be above committing murder.

Corey, Sam, and Marcus leave, promising to update me on whatever they learn from the electronic surveillance. Once they do, Laurie says, "You're not happy."

I nod. "Not terribly. I should have been consulted before all this took place. Surveillance devices in a truck?"

"I know. It's my fault, and I'm sorry. You were in jury selection, and they had the opportunity and needed an answer."

"It could have gone wrong. Mitchell would have been alerted to the fact that we are watching him. It could still go wrong."

"Yes."

"But they did amazing work," I say, admitting the obvious.

"Yes, they did. We'll keep you in the loop from now on."

"Thank you. Now, woman, get me my blueberry muffin."

We leave a mark wherever we go, whatever we do, and whatever we say."

Steinkamp is beginning his opening statement to the jury. He has a pleasant conversational style, as if he is talking to his neighbors and friends, and for all I know, he is.

The gallery is packed; this is still a major story in the area. The sentiment has remained on the side of the prosecution; it will take some guts for jurors to vote to acquit.

He continues, "It's a fact of life: every move we make, every word we utter, has an effect on the world. Sometimes it's minor, sometimes it's of great significance.

"What you are doing today is in the latter category; it is hugely significant. The decisions you make in this courtroom will change the world; certainly for this defendant, and certainly for our society. You will leave your mark on the world, as will I, as will Mr. Carpenter, as will Judge Pressley.

"But we also leave another kind of mark, everywhere we go, and that is also what this trial is about. We leave a physical trail: we leave our DNA.

"Science has come a long way in the area of DNA detection and analysis. But the fact is that if you touched that railing on the way to taking your seat in this jury box, then your DNA is on that railing. Forensics people, if they were so inclined, could come in and prove conclusively that you were here."

Steinkamp points to Matt Jantzen, sitting between Charlie Tilton and me at the defense table.

"Matthew Jantzen left his mark the night he broke into a house and murdered Tina Welker and Peter Charkin. It did not take any new scientific advances to determine that fact. Peter Charkin made the forensic job an easy one by struggling with his attacker, by actually drawing his blood while fighting for his life.

"Matthew Jantzen's blood was found on Peter Charkin's right hand. Mr. Charkin had lost his struggle; he had been beaten and then tied to a chair. His friend Tina Welker was tied to another chair. They were both shot at close range in the head. Cold-blooded murders if ever there were any.

"But Mr. Charkin left a message for us in death: He served up the identity of his killer on a platter. He had the blood of his attacker on his hand. It is more incriminating than if he had coaxed his killer into signing a confession. Confessions can be forged; blood DNA cannot.

"You will hear other evidence that will be consistent with Mr. Jantzen's guilt, and it is my obligation to offer it to you. But the DNA is really all you need to know.

"Judge Pressley will instruct you as to your obligations in this matter, and one of the things you will hear about is reasonable doubt. There is no other reasonable explanation for Matthew Jantzen's blood being on the defendant than his having been the killer.

"Mr. Carpenter will try to deflect and point you in a different direction, but he will not be able to change this key fact, and all I ask is that you focus on it.

"When you do, I am confident you will vote to convict

Matthew Jantzen of the brutal murders of Tina Welker and Peter Charkin.

"Thank you for listening, and thank you for your service."

I think Steinkamp's homing in on the DNA was the correct approach. The DNA is the key to his case, and to talk about it as just one piece of evidence among many is to diminish it. If you're trying to convince someone of Tom Brady's greatness, you don't babble about his ability to sidestep the rush or run the quarterback sneak. You talk about how great the guy is at passing the damn ball.

In this case, the DNA is the damn ball.

I accept Judge Pressley's offer to give our opening statement now, rather than at the beginning of the defense case. I have made this same decision in every trial I have been a part of. The jury has heard from Steinkamp, and they are about to hear his entire case. I can't let that happen without them knowing that there is another side to the story.

"Ladies and gentlemen, Mr. Steinkamp's case is based on science, in this case DNA science. He's relying on it totally; he considers it incapable of error. He so strongly believes in it, that he is ready to take away a man's freedom, for many years if not the rest of his life, based on what the science says.

"This may surprise you, but I also believe in science, perhaps as strongly as does Mr. Steinkamp. Of course, I don't consider it infallible; in fact scientists don't either. They are frequently adjusting their theories based on new evidence and discoveries; doing so is entirely consistent with the scientific process.

"But I want you to understand one thing as you hear this evidence. Science may well be correct the overwhelming percentage of the time, but people are not. Science rarely makes mistakes; people make them all the time.

"Who collected this evidence? Who transferred it? Who stored it? Who tested it? People. And people make errors, sometimes deliberate, more often accidental. They don't have to be intentional mistakes, and we are not alleging such misconduct. But when you are convicting someone of murder, you better be very sure that what they are telling you is right.

"They cannot hide behind the science when everything else points in the other direction. Matt Jantzen has an impeccable record. He has never been accused of a crime, never even been a suspect, or, as they say now, a 'person of interest.'

"He did not know the victims, yet all of a sudden he breaks into their house and commits a vicious double murder? And then two years later acts in such a way that would have been sure to draw the police to him?

"You'll hear it all, and I believe you will come to the conclusion that none of it makes sense, that Matthew Jantzen is sitting here because people make mistakes.

"You will come to understand that in bringing these charges, the State of Maine has made a beauty of a mistake.

"The good news is that you will have the power to correct it."

Steinkamp's first witness is Vivian Kramer, a vice president at origin.com.

It is the DNA ancestry service that both Matt Jantzen and his sister, Mary Patrick, sent their DNA to, which ultimately is how the police came to arrest Matt. Steinkamp's goal is simply to set the scene for the jury by describing how the police conducted their investigation.

Ms. Kramer is young and eager and seems smart, exactly as I picture everyone who works for a company whose name ends in *.com.*

I think it's a mistake for Steinkamp to introduce this testimony, an unforced error. I hope it's not the last one.

Steinkamp has Kramer describe the service that the company provides, which she is all too happy to do.

"We tell people all the things they can learn from their DNA, everything from predispositions to certain illnesses to various likes and dislikes they might have."

"Can you give an example?"

"Sure. When I had my sample analyzed, among many other things it said that I would have a weakness for chocolate." She smiles broadly. "Wow, were they ever right about that."

"What else does your service tell customers?"

"All about their ancestors. Where they came from, by percentage . . . that's probably the thing people most want to know. Some people will think they are of a certain descent, only to find out they are completely wrong. It can be amazing."

"Anything else?"

She nods. "Definitely. We can also tell people about relatives whose samples are in the system. Sometimes they are people that don't even realize they are related. Many people have found close relatives that way. Adopted children have found their biological parents in the same manner."

"Did there come a time when the defendant submitted a DNA sample to your company?" Steinkamp asks.

"Yes, sir."

"And you provided the type of analysis you just described?"

"Yes."

"Did it show any relatives that you could identify?"

"Yes, a woman named Mary Patrick. She was shown to be a half-sibling, meaning they had one parent in common."

"Thank you. No further questions."

I stand up for my first cross-examination of the trial. "Ms. Kramer, did your company approach Mr. Jantzen and ask him to send in a DNA sample?"

"No, certainly not. We would never do that."

"He did so of his own free will?"

"Yes."

"Did you compensate him for doing so? Was he paid for his efforts?"

"Of course not."

"Did he pay you? Is there a fee for your service?"

"Yes, he paid the fee."

I introduce the agreement form between the company and their customers and ask her to read the part about making the results public. After she gets through all the legalese, I ask her to put it in layman's terms.

"Our customers have a choice as to whether to make their profiles public. If they choose to, then other people can see it and perhaps make a connection to them."

"Do most people consent to that?"

"Well more than half, yes."

"So had Mr. Jantzen not voluntarily signed up, and had he not voluntarily consented to this provision, his information would not have been made public?"

"That is correct."

"And in that case, would law enforcement have had access to it?"

"They would not."

I introduce four newspaper articles, three from various areas in Maine and one from the *Boston Globe.* I ask her to scan them and verify that they are from around the time of the murders, and that they all reveal that DNA evidence was found at the scene.

Once she's done, I ask, "Just to reconfirm, had Mr. Jantzen not consented, law enforcement would never have seen his DNA results?"

"That's right."

"So Mr. Jantzen voluntarily read and signed a document which allowed his DNA to be viewed by law enforcement?"

Steinkamp stands. "Objection. Asked and answered."

"Sustained," Judge Pressley says.

I smile. "I'm sorry, Your Honor, I liked the answer so much I wanted to hear it again."

"Be careful, Mr. Carpenter."

"Yes, Your Honor." I turn back to Ms. Kramer. "By the way, you testified that Mr. Jantzen sent in his DNA voluntarily."

"Yes."

"I guess I want to understand how you know he sent it at all?"

"I don't understand what you mean," she says, genuinely confused. "We received it."

"But how can you be sure that it was actually Mr. Jantzen that sent it?"

"He signed the form."

"Oh, I didn't realize it came with a signature and everything. You had his signature on file, so you were able to compare it?"

"No."

"Is it possible that someone else sent it in using his name, and signing it for him?"

"I suppose it's possible. But I don't know why he would do that."

"Do you know why someone who committed a crime and left his DNA on the scene would send that DNA out into the public, where the police could see it?"

Steinkamp objects before she can answer, and Judge Pressley sustains it.

"While we're at it, Ms. Kramer, is it possible it wasn't Mr. Jantzen's DNA at all?"

"Mr. Carpenter, we just analyze the samples that we are sent. I'm afraid we're not in a position to question things like that."

I smile. "I understand. That's the kind of thing juries are for. No further questions."

Nice job this morning," Charlie Tilton says.

We've just sat down for a quick lunch at a coffee shop down the block from the courthouse. It is the first place I've been at in Maine, gas stations included, that doesn't serve lobster rolls.

"Steinkamp blew it," I say. "He didn't have to put her on the stand; what the hell is the difference how the police came to have Matt's DNA? He could have had the homicide detective mention it when he testifies; it would have been two sentences."

"Yeah, he surprised me. He teed it up for you."

"So he's usually better than that?"

Tilton nods. "In my experience, yes. But this is a big case for him, big publicity, going up against a New Jersey lawyer. . . ."

"New York." They've all said New York so much that I might as well embrace it.

"Whatever. He's overthinking it. But he'll settle down, and he's got some good lawyers working with him. They'll give it to him straight."

"That's what I figured. And at the end of the day, it doesn't matter. They have the DNA they took from Matt since he's been in custody. It matches the blood on Charkin's hand, so the website DNA is of no importance."

"It gave them probable cause to make the arrest," Tilton points out.

"True."

"You think Matt did it?"

It's been a while since I've thought about it; I've been so focused on finding the killer that I haven't taken time to reflect on whether I'm representing him.

"No. I don't. It's partially the things we're learning about Charkin, but it's also the way the murders were committed. The cold-blooded way the gun was put to the heads of people who were probably begging for their lives. I don't know Matt that well, but I just can't connect him to the person that could have pulled that trigger."

"Maybe I'm just buying into your big-city bullshit, but I don't think he did it either. The problem is that if I was on that jury, I'd vote to convict."

"I haven't worked my magic yet."

Tilton smiles. "Good. That will give me something to look forward to."

Steinkamp's next witness is Walt Kapler, who works as a bartender at Parker's Pub, in Nobleboro. Steinkamp starts by having Kapler state his occupation and his place of employment.

"Were you working there two years ago, at the time of the murders?"

"Yeah, I've been working at Parker's for nine years." Kapler smiles. "My career has sort of hit a plateau."

"Did I ask you to drive from the pub to the house where the murders took place?"

Kapler nods. "Yes, and I did it. There are two ways to do it, so I tried both of them. They took just about the same amount of time."

"How long did it take?"

"About seven minutes."

"Have you ever spoken to the defendant, Matthew Jantzen?"

"Oh, sure. Many times."

"Under what circumstances?"

"He used to come in the bar a lot. I wouldn't say he was a regular, but he was in maybe once a week, or a little less."

Steinkamp introduces a credit card receipt as evidence and gets Kapler to identify it as Matt's and confirm it is from the night of the murder.

"What time was it signed?"

"Nine forty-seven P.M."

"Nine forty-seven," Steinkamp repeats. He does so for no other reason than the hope that the jury will remember it, since it is within an hour of the estimated time of death. Kapler can't testify as to the time of death, but Steinkamp will be sure to make the connection later.

"In your experience with Mr. Jantzen and other customers, is it common for them to leave soon after they pay their bill?"

"Sure, if you're not going to drink anymore, what are you there for, you know?"

Steinkamp turns the witness over to me. "Mr. Kapler," I ask, "were you working at the bar the night of the murders?"

"I don't remember. The bar doesn't keep records that far back and I sure don't keep my calendars."

"How many nights a week were you working back then?" I know all these answers from the interview turned over to us in discovery.

"Three or four, depending on the week."

"So it's about a fifty percent chance that you were there that night?"

"I'd say that's right, yeah."

"But if you were there, you don't remember anything about it specifically, correct?"

He nods. "Right."

"Did Matt Jantzen usually come in and sit alone?"

"No, they had a pretty big group. They were buddies."

"Did they ever leave drunk and get into their cars and drive?"

"No way." Kapler describes how they would always have a designated driver who didn't drink, and how one person always paid for everybody. They alternated paying.

"Did the person who paid act as the designated driver?"

"No, the guy who paid always drank. I guess he got his money's worth."

"So considering the size of this bill, based on your experience is it likely that Mr. Jantzen did not drive there that night?"

Steinkamp objects that the witness could not testify to something he had no direct knowledge about, but Judge Pressley lets him answer.

"I never thought of that, but he probably didn't drive."

"Were there ever women at the bar?"

"Sure. Lots of times."

"And sometimes they would form couples with the guys, and maybe a man and woman would leave together?"

"Oh, yeah. Happened all the time."

"So it's possible that Matt Jantzen left the bar with a woman that night?"

Kapler nods. "Possible. Yeah."

"But you don't know one way or the other, because you don't even remember being there yourself."

"Right."

I frown and feign annoyance that I even had to deal with such a ridiculous witness. I'm a good annoyance-feigner. "No further questions."

This trial feels like we are slowly being dragged to the edge of a cliff.

The first two witnesses have not gone badly; one could argue that we have not suffered any real damage and that we've even scored some points. But anyone on our side taking heart in that would be buying into an illusion, because it doesn't matter.

What matters is the DNA, and that testimony will be coming fairly soon; it's just over the edge of that cliff. Steinkamp has it cocked and loaded, ready to use whenever he is in the mood.

I know where this is going; it is headed to a certain conviction. It's as certain as the ending of a movie I have seen before. We will have fought the good fight, and we will have lost. Then we can throw up our hands and say we did all that we could, and Matt Jantzen can go to jail for the rest of his life, convicted of murders I don't believe he committed.

All we have now are Peter Charkin's connections to two violent worlds. One is Donnelly and drugs; Charkin was taking them, and his buddy and employer Mitchell was tied up in a neat bow with Donnelly and his dealer lieutenant Carmody.

The other is McCaskill and the Liberators militia. We know and can demonstrate the connection is real; we originally got it from the police reports in the discovery documents, from back before they decided that Matt Jantzen was the guilty party.

We don't know much more about the militia side, except that the FBI has an active investigation that is causing them to worry a lot. I can't worry about their worry; it only interests me if it has something to do with our case.

But because the trial result seems inevitable, we need to take action on both fronts. We have to do more than show that Charkin hung out with bad guys; we have to demonstrate that he did bad things himself, and that's what got him killed.

It's easy to decide to be aggressive; this is that rare time that everyone on the team shares that goal. The difficult part is to figure out the form for that aggression. To that end, everybody gathers in Laurie's and my suite one evening after the day in court to discuss it and make our plans.

Corey, Laurie, Sam, Marcus, and I hash it out. It's my case, so I have the final word, but I am conflicted. There simply do not seem to be any promising options, but we wind up with what seems to be the best of a weak bunch.

Laurie and I are going to confront Danny McCaskill again. We will make vague threats about knowing of his connection to Gavin Helms, and about how the militia was supplying Charkin with cash infusions. We'll throw in the FBI's imminent plan to come down on both of them. We'll tell him that revealing all he knows, including about Charkin's murder, is the only chance he'll have to save himself.

It's 80 percent bullshit, and the rest is speculation, but at least we'll be doing something.

Corey and Marcus have an even vaguer assignment. They're heading for Vermont, where the cell phone GPS places Gavin Helms's location. Google Earth shows it to be in the middle of nowhere, and we want to at least find out what is going on there, and who Helms is with.

What they do with that information will be up to Corey and Marcus, depending on what they find. In a perfect world they can get Helms or others to talk about Charkin.

Once again it seems like a fantasy that we'll find out anything to tie to the murders and our case, but the more stuff we can learn, the more I can throw on the jury wall, hoping something sticks.

Nobody is terribly happy with these plans, least of all Sam Willis. Like always, he wants to be out in the field, shooting bad guys and taking no prisoners. He'll stay behind and be in charge of communications, including monitoring the electronic surveillance on the truck that makes the deliveries to the Maine Lighthouse brewery.

I wish I could trade places with him.

The trial day today is going to feel even longer than usual.

Usually, when the prosecution is presenting its case, a day seems to last for a little over a week, maybe longer. Today will feel like about a month, because after court Laurie and I are going to confront Danny McCaskill.

The last time I saw McCaskill, he just about threatened to beat the hell out of Charlie Tilton and me. He's less likely to pull it off this time because Laurie is tougher than Charlie and me put together. She also carries a gun, which can be useful in such situations.

But I still don't like confrontations that might end in violence, and I especially hate the ones where I have to rely on my wife for protection. But it is what it is, and I am what I am. That doesn't mean I don't dread it.

Steinkamp's first witness is Sergeant Robert Prentice of the Lincoln County Sheriff's Office. He was one of the first officers on the scene at Tina Welker's house the night of the murders.

Once Steinkamp has established that Prentice has fifteen years of exemplary service in the department, he asks how Prentice came to be at the house.

"A neighbor called nine-one-one. He reported that shots were fired, although he wasn't sure where they came from."

The neighbor was originally on Steinkamp's witness list, but he apparently won't be called. Apparently he has learned his lesson not to overdo it.

"What did you do when you arrived on the scene?"

"We went to the neighbor's house, and he informed us as to the general direction from where he heard the shots. I called in four more officers, and we fanned out and checked each house."

"Was Tina Welker's house one of the ones you went to?"

Prentice nods. "It was the first house that my partner and I checked. The front door was slightly ajar, and no one answered the bell when we rang repeatedly. We were concerned that someone might be hurt inside, so we went in."

Prentice was careful to voice that concern so that it wouldn't be considered an illegal entry. Therefore any evidence found within would be admissible.

"What did you find when you went inside?"

"Two deceased adults, later identified as Tina Welker and Peter Charkin. They were tied to chairs and shot through the head, one shot each."

"What did you do next?"

"We confirmed that the adults were deceased. Then we called in backup and set about determining that the killer was no longer in the house. Once we did that, we secured the scene and waited for Robbery-Homicide and forensics to arrive."

"So no one interfered with any evidence? No contamination?"

"None. The scene was secured and locked down until forensics got there."

"Did you notice any other injuries on the deceased other than from the gunshots?"

Prentice nods. "Mr. Charkin appeared to have facial injuries, bruises or lacerations. It was hard for me to tell because of all the blood from the gunshot wounds, and I didn't want to get too close for fear of contaminating possible evidence."

Steinkamp displays the crime-scene photographs on a screen that has been set up. They are obviously horrible, which is why Steinkamp wanted them shown.

The jury sees the two people, tied up and helpless, with their heads blown open and blood everywhere. Not only would they vote to convict Jantzen at this moment; they would hang him themselves in the courtroom if the judge would let them.

Steinkamp turns the witness over to me. He didn't cause me much damage, except for creating the general impression that the area remained sterile and untouched. So I will just ask a few questions and get out.

"Sergeant Prentice, you said that you confirmed the two victims were deceased before you did anything else?"

"That's correct."

"How did you do that?"

"I felt for a pulse on their necks."

"You also said that you didn't want to get too close to the bodies, because doing so might contaminate evidence. How did you go about feeling their necks without getting close?"

"That's all I did. I felt their necks and moved away."

"So getting close might contaminate the evidence, and you did get close? You just didn't get close repeatedly? Is that your testimony?"

"I needed to confirm that they were deceased."

"That would be a good answer if I had asked what you needed to confirm. But that's not what I asked. I asked if you touched them, even though you thought that would risk contaminating the evidence."

"Yes, I did. I had to make sure they were not still alive and in need of medical attention."

"You saw what we just saw in those photographs and you thought they might have been just wounded?"

"You never know."

"Thank you, Sergeant. No further questions."

After lunch Judge Pressley announces that a juror has a medical issue. The juror expects it to be resolved this afternoon, but if not, an alternate will replace that juror.

Court is adjourned for the day, which is fine with me. I need the time to obsess over tonight.

The first thing that Corey and Marcus discovered was that Google Earth was right.

The area that GPS had identified as the location of Gavin Helms's phone was, in fact, in the middle of nowhere. It was a wooded nowhere, with small paths cut out that may once have been used for hiking, but were now mostly overrun. Corey and Marcus were hopeful that one led to wherever Helms was staying, but there was no way to be sure.

"They must have their own cell tower," Corey said, noticing that his phone had good service, even though this was a desolate area. Marcus didn't respond, which was no surprise; he had said maybe ten indecipherable words the entire way.

Corey was nominally in charge, and he signaled that Marcus should go down one path, while Corey would take an adjacent one. There was no way to determine how far the paths would diverge, so it was a risk. With no way to communicate with each other, it was far from an ideal situation, but Corey still felt it was better to take separate paths.

"We meet back here in an hour," Corey said, and Marcus nodded his assent.

Corey was glad that he had not brought Simon Garfunkel. This was just a reconnaissance mission, and it would have been rough terrain for a dog heading into his senior years. It made Corey feel more alone, though, since he and Simon had been partners for almost eight years and had faced a great deal together.

Corey had been walking for about ten minutes when he heard the gunshots. There was no mistaking them; the sound blasted through the dead silence that preceded them.

For a moment he feared that Marcus had been discovered and was caught in a gunfight, or worse, but then felt relieved as the sounds continued. The number and pace of the shots indicated target practice rather than shots fired with any urgency or under duress.

Corey judged that the shots came from just a few hundred yards ahead. A major worry was that he and Marcus were heading for the target range itself; the bullets might be coming in their direction, and they might walk into them.

"Do not move another inch," the voice said, coming from Corey's right side. He looked and saw a tall, well-built man, no more than twenty-five years old, pointing a rifle at him.

The first thing Corey thought was that not bringing Simon was a major, life-threatening mistake. Simon would have detected the guy's presence earlier, alerted Corey, and most likely disabled the guy with extreme prejudice. "Okay," Corey said. "But you don't need the rifle. I'm not doing anything wrong."

"What are you doing here?"

"Just out hiking and scouting some land. I'm thinking of buying out here."

"Bullshit. Let's go."

"Where?"

"To meet some people who will be interested in hearing what you have to say. And they will get you to say it."

The man with the rifle took one step toward Corey, motioning with the rifle for him to continue down the path. At that moment a large tree fell and hit the man on the side of the head. Actually, if he had had the time to register the event before he instantly lost consciousness, he would have assumed it was a large tree, but it was Marcus Clark's forearm.

Corey's first thought was the hope the guy was not dead. After that his cop instinct kicked in: They were on private property and had attacked someone who probably had the right to be there. That he had held a rifle on Corey was an extenuating circumstance.

Corey felt for the guy's pulse and was relieved to discover one. Now it came time to decide whether to go back or forward, and Marcus silently made that decision for them, as he started along the trail toward the gunshots. They had come this far, Marcus was not giving up now.

They had no way to tie up the unconscious guy, so all Corey could do was take the guy's rifle and hope he didn't wake up until they accomplished whatever they needed to. He didn't look as if consciousness was imminent.

In another five minutes they came to a clearing and could see the large cabin and the three men at the makeshift target range. Fortunately, Corey and Marcus were to the south, and the men were firing east to west.

Two men were firing in what appeared to be a competition, while the other watched, also holding a handgun and no doubt awaiting his turn. They were talking and laughing, obviously with no idea that they were being watched, or that one of their colleagues was in never-never land.

There was no sense in going in, Corey realized. The men were not doing anything illegal and likely had a right to be there. Nor did Corey and Marcus have anything approaching any legal jurisdiction. Added to that, the men were armed and intervention made no sense.

Corey had had the foresight to bring a camera with a telephoto lens, and he took pictures of the three men and their surroundings. He also checked his phone app for the accurate latitude and longitude of the cabin.

They left the way they came, passing the guard still crumpled on the ground. Corey felt for the guy's pulse again, found it to be stronger, and was hopeful that he would soon awaken. If not, the others would no doubt find him.

Or not. Corey didn't care that much either way.

L aurie is annoyingly calm about this.

I've told her that McCaskill is a large person who does not take kindly to being questioned. He is apparently violent and dangerous, two qualities that I am not fond of in anyone not named Marcus.

Laurie has dealt with people like McCaskill in her former police-officer life, and she just relies on her training. And her smarts. And her gun, if necessary. I rely on my wits, which is to say I am unarmed.

But that she's not nervous doesn't mean she isn't careful. We lay out exactly how we will approach McCaskill, verbally as well as physically. We talk about what we want to find out, and how we will go about accomplishing our goal.

It is extremely unlikely that this effort will help in Matt Jantzen's defense. But I see no possibility it will be counterproductive, so it is worth a try.

We are going to play to our strengths, meaning that I will be doing most of the talking, and she will be doing all of the protecting. We go over it one more time on the way there, but adjustments will have to be made, depending on what McCaskill has to say.

We pull up about three doors down from McCaskill's house.

That is so that he will have less time to see us coming. We'd like to surprise him to the degree that we can.

As we get out of the car, I take one last look at my phone. Laurie sees me doing that and asks, "Still no word from Corey and Marcus?"

"No."

I'm surprised that we haven't heard from them; they should have gotten to Vermont quite a while ago. I'm not terribly worried, and I doubt that Laurie is either. Corey is capable of handling himself, and with Marcus by his side, I would be confident if they were invading North Korea.

McCaskill's car is in the driveway, a sign that he is home. Another good sign is that we can hear music coming from inside the house. He plays his music loudly; I can't make out what it is, but it's a good bet it's not a show tune.

I ring the bell, but McCaskill doesn't answer, possibly because of the music. Another ring gets a similar lack of response. I'm willing to abort and go home, but Laurie is of a different mind, and she pounds on the door.

No answer.

Laurie doesn't give up easily. Without saying anything, she walks down the steps and into the driveway, looking in windows along the way. I sure as hell don't want to be alone on the porch if McCaskill finally opens the door, so I follow her.

She's near the back of the house and I'm about twenty feet behind when she calls out, "Andy."

As I get closer, I see that her gun is drawn and she is scanning the area. Finally I am close enough to see what she sees. The back door to the house is open and McCaskill is lying prone, half in and half out of the doorway, his back covered in blood.

Laurie has her phone out and is talking into it. "I want to report a shooting." She provides the address and her name. "I believe deceased, but I am about to confirm that. . . . Yes, we are at the scene. Please alert the officers that I am a licensed private investigator carrying a weapon. . . . We will remain here."

The only words I am able to get out at the moment are "Holy shit."

t takes four hours for Laurie and me to get back to the hotel. The police at the scene took their time with us, questioning us separately and then getting us to make our written statements.

We'd probably still be there had not Agent Nichols arrived on the scene, more evidence that the FBI is interested in McCaskill and the operations of the group to which he belonged.

Nichols vouched for us to the cops, which hastened our departure. But before we left, he said, "We had an information-sharing agreement."

"You must be kidding," I said. "We haven't heard a word from you."

"I have nothing of interest to your case. But you're apparently very involved in mine."

"I do have one news flash for you, actually. McCaskill is dead."

"Don't mess with me, Carpenter."

"Wouldn't dream of it. But I may have something for you tomorrow."

"What? There's an urgency to this, Carpenter."

"Tomorrow. If I have something, I will call you."

Three messages are on each of our phones from Corey, telling us to call him so that we can meet tonight. He has a lot to tell us and wants to hear what happened on our end. We call and head back to the hotel, where he, Marcus, and Sam are waiting for us.

Laurie and I describe the fun evening we had. After we do so, Laurie says, "My guess is that McCaskill knew his killer and did not consider him a threat until it was too late."

"Why?" I ask, since she hadn't mentioned that earlier.

"Because there was no sign of forced entry at the front door, and I didn't see any open windows, at least on the side we were on. There is a nearby neighbor on the other side, so if the killer was going to come through a window, it would have been where we were.

"Unlikely that he came in the back door, because McCaskill was running out that way. He wouldn't have been running towards the killer."

When we're done, Corey describes his and Marcus's time in Vermont, which makes our evening sound like a fun walk in the park.

When they're done, Laurie asks, "What's your sense of it?"

"I think it was more of a home base rather than anything else. I doubt they were doing anything there other than biding their time and waiting, though I don't know what they were waiting for."

"So you saw four guys, including the one Marcus decked?"

"Yes, but there were likely others. There could have been more in the cabin, but there were almost certainly more perimeter guards. That place could have been approached from all sides; it's likely a number of guards each had their sector."

"He was unlucky that you chose his area," Laurie says.

"I'm sorry we ran into him," Corey says, "because now that they know they've been discovered, they're going to leave. They might be gone already."

The general sense in the room is that we're getting somewhere, a sense that I don't share. I'm finding the whole thing a bit depressing.

We discovered a dead militia guy, and Corey and Marcus discovered a bunch of live ones. It will give me a great story to tell Matt Jantzen when I go visiting him during his life prison sentence, but it does not give me a story to tell the jury.

Sam has taken the digital photos that Corey shot and printed them out. The faces of the men are clear and distinct, but I don't have the slightest idea who they are.

"Please email them to Agent Nichols on my behalf. Ask him if these people mean anything to him."

"Will do," Sam says.

"Thanks. I've got an early court date in the morning, so Laurie and I are going to walk the dogs and go to bed."

can see that Matt Jantzen is upset when Chris Myers takes the stand.

I had told him that Myers was on Steinkamp's witness list, but it is still upsetting to Matt to see a person he considers a friend testifying for the prosecution.

"Mr. Myers, do you and the defendant know each other?"

Myers nods. "Since we were little kids. Matt moved into our neighborhood when we were both five years old."

"And you went to school together?"

"Yes, both grammar school and high school."

"Would you describe yourself as good friends?"

Myers does not look at Matt; he hasn't looked at him since sitting down, and I suspect that won't change. "Until today, yes."

"You intend to tell the truth today, do you not?"

"I do."

"When was the last time you saw the defendant, prior to to-day?"

"About two years ago."

"Please describe your relationship back then."

Myers thinks for a bit. "We hung out together. I mean, we were part of a group, but we'd also do things just the two of us, or with one other person. You know, fishing, playing pickup basketball, that kind of stuff."

"What happened two years ago to change that?"

"Well, for one thing, Matt left Maine."

"Did that take you by surprise?"

"Sort of; by then I knew that something was going on."

"What do you mean by that?" Steinkamp asks, as if he doesn't already know.

"He had been acting strangely, not himself. He still hung out sometimes, but he was like only half there."

"Did you ask him why?"

Myers nods. "A bunch of times; I asked if I could help, but he just cut me off and said nothing was wrong. I mean, he had lost his mother not that long before, and his girlfriend broke up with him. Then another one of our friends, Carl Blanchard, died of cancer. I figured it was all of that, so I didn't push him."

"Do you remember where you were the night of the murder?"

"I can't be sure, but we were probably at Parker's . . . that's a pub in Nobleboro. We went there a lot."

"Did you ever talk about the murders with the defendant?"

"I'm sure I must have; it's all anyone was talking about for a few days. And we knew Tina."

"You knew Tina Welker?"

"Yes."

"Did the defendant know her?"

"I can't say for sure, but I would assume he did. She hung out with all of us sometimes."

"So two weeks after the murder he left Maine, where he had lived all his life?"

"Yes."

"Did he ever say why?"

"Not to me."

"Thank you, Mr. Myers."

I frown slightly as I stand, as if annoyed that I have to deal with this nonsense. "Mr. Myers, you said that Mr. Jantzen had lost his mother and a good friend?"

"Yes."

"And his girlfriend broke up with him?"

"Yes."

"And you were puzzled as to why he seemed out of sorts?"

"Well, I figured it was all of that."

"Good figuring."

Steinkamp objects that I am badgering the witness. Judge Pressley sustains and admonishes me to be careful. They're clearly touchy here in Maine.

"You were close friends with Mr. Jantzen from the time you were five until two years ago?"

"Yes."

"You did favors for each other, like friends do?"

"Yes."

"Did you ever bail him out of jail?"

"No."

"To your knowledge, was he ever arrested?"

"Not that I know of."

"Ever in a fight? Ever violent?"

"Not that I know of."

"Did you ever see him with a handgun?"

"No."

"Ever commit a robbery? A home invasion?"

"Not to my knowledge."

"Ever worry that he would shoot somebody?"

"No."

"You said that he might have known Tina Welker; did you ever hear them argue?"

"No."

"Ever hear him say a bad word about her?"

"No."

"Ever hear him say any word about her at all?"

"Not that I remember."

"Thank you. No further questions."

I put on my annoyed frown as I head back to the defense table, this time coupling it with a slight, disapproving shake of the head. I am the De Niro of defense attorneys.

J udge Pressley surprises me after lunch by announcing that she has important business to attend to, and she is adjourning court for the day.

I'm not unhappy about it; the longer the trial takes, the more time for divine intervention to somehow give me a case to present to the jury.

As Charlie and I are leaving, I see Agent Nichols standing in the rear of the courtroom, obviously waiting for me. "You and I have to talk."

I'm about to say something sarcastic and obnoxious, but based on Nichols's face and tone, this is probably not the right time for it. Instead I say good-bye to Charlie and follow Nichols to his car, parked in a spot reserved for court personnel.

Once we're in the front seat, I ask, "Where are we going?"

"Nowhere. We're going to talk right here."

"Are you the important business that Judge Pressley had to attend to?"

"Think of it as intergovernmental cooperation. You sent me photographs. I want to know everything there is to know about them, starting right now."

I can be intimidated and scared by a lot of things. Tough guys, guns, mice, spiders, and Laurie when she's pissed at me are just some of them. But words are not on that list, no matter who is speaking them. If Cindy Spodek described me accurately, she would have told Nichols that, along with that I am a pain in the ass.

"Sorry, that's not how this is going to work," I say.

"What the hell does that mean?"

"It means I have a client to defend. I won't say that's all I care about, but it is sure as hell in first position. So if you want to know what I know, then first you'll tell me what the hell is going on."

"This has nothing whatsoever to do with your client."

"It turns out that the way this works is I'm the judge of what impacts my client. And he is accused of murdering someone knee-deep in the drug world and the world of people who hang out in the woods taking target practice, people who are obviously of intense interest to the FBI.

"So you go first, Agent Nichols. . . . I'd bet that Cindy Spodek told you that at the end of the day I could be trusted. This is the time to put it to the test."

Nichols hesitates, as if trying to decide what to do. It's all bullshit, and it's not as good an acting performance as I put on in the courtroom. He and his people had to anticipate this situation and would have decided what to do.

The good news for me is that they don't have a choice.

He takes a piece of paper out of his inside pocket and unfolds it. It's one of the photos of the three men in Vermont that Sam emailed to him. He points to the man watching the other two shoot.

"That's Darrin Jeffrey."

Nichols is talking about the militia leader said to have been killed eighteen months ago. "He looks pretty lively for a dead guy."

"We never believed he was killed; the whole thing was a setup. But he effectively disappeared, until you somehow got a picture of him."

"Why is he so important to you?"

"These groups have expanded exponentially because of social media. Some of them have gone from Second Amendment people who see themselves as fighting for freedom to full-blown loonies that see a conspiracy under every rock. Their ideology is causing damage to everyone and everything that doesn't agree with their cause, even though they can't agree on what the hell their cause of the day is.

"It's all done online in various forms. Some is out in the open, some on the dark web, some encrypted, but most not. Between the Bureau and all the other agencies under Homeland Security, we've got an army of people tracking it all.

"A while back, more than two years ago, we started picking up some chatter about a major event that they were planning. We believe they are going to detonate a significant device; we don't know exactly what kind of device or why they have waited so long. But they clearly consider it a game changer. One thing is certain: Darrin Jeffrey is at the center of it all."

"Did they kill McCaskill?"

Nichols nods, then hesitates. "McCaskill was an FBI informant; or at least we believed that he was."

"He was good at it. When I questioned him, he threatened me."

"You're easy to dislike."

"What do you mean you 'believed that he was'?"

"He was what they call in the movies a double agent. We learned that when you said he called Helms. He had not revealed a knowledge of Helms's whereabouts to us. We were in the process of deciding what to do with him when he turned up dead."

"So you didn't monitor his phone because you thought he was on your side. That's why you didn't know he was in contact with Helms."

"Right."

"But why would they kill him if he was on their side?"

Nichols shrugs. "No way to be sure. Maybe they didn't fully trust him, or maybe they were just cleaning up loose ends. It speaks to the urgency of this."

"Where did Peter Charkin fit in?"

Nichols shrugs. "We don't know, but he was part of the chatter; he was definitely involved. Once they decided they didn't need him anymore, they got rid of him."

"And framed Matt Jantzen."

"I have no information to back that up, so I can't help you in court. . . . Your turn."

I tell him that we had located Helms in Vermont, and he stops me. "How did you do that?"

I'm not about to throw Sam under the bus, so I say, "Let's just say that if you used our methods, you would have to get a warrant. We are, as you can imagine, desperate to tie Charkin to bad guys capable of murder, so two of my investigators went up there to see what they could find out. That's how they got the photographs."

"You'll show us where the place is." It's a statement, certainly not a question.

"Absolutely; I can even give you the exact coordinates. But I'm afraid it will be of limited value to you."

"Why?"

"Our investigators were discovered by a guard with a rifle. They dispatched him."

"He's dead?"

"No, but there's no doubt it took him a while to wake up,

and he'll be drooling for the foreseeable future. I would assume that Jeffrey would have taken the event as a sign to abandon the location."

"Your investigators were stupid."

That annoys me. "Which part? The part where they prevented themselves from getting killed, or the part where they found somebody that you couldn't find for eighteen months?"

Nichols and I drive in our separate cars back to the hotel. I call ahead and have Corey waiting to give him the exact coordinates of the cabin in Vermont, and to describe the terrain and surrounding area.

I go to our room to update Laurie, take the dogs for a walk, and think about what, if anything, this new knowledge does for our case.

When it comes to murderous bad guys that Peter Charkin was involved with, we have an embarrassment of riches.

It's all I can do to pick a most likely candidate as to which group killed him and Tina Welker.

Until recently, the leader heading into the stretch was the drug connection, Jerry Donnelly in charge. Charkin was clearly involved with them; not only was he using the product, but he seems to have been tied in with Mike Mitchell. Mitchell has a significant business relationship with Donnelly, no doubt an illegal one, but the details of which I haven't been able to figure out.

We haven't made any progress in that regard because Sam reports that the truck we have our surveillance equipment in has not moved. My fear is that they have switched trucks, rendering us blind to their movements.

A candidate coming up fast on the outside is the group headed up by Darrin Jeffrey. Something big is going on, something that Nichols said Charkin had at least a small part of. The killing of McCaskill shows that not only is this group capable of cold-blooded murder, but it also implies an urgency to whatever is going on.

I probably lean toward the Donnelly connection as being responsible for the murders. Charkin, especially because of the connection with Mitchell, seems to have had the potential to be significant on some level to the operation.

On the Darrin Jeffrey side, I don't know how Charkin could have been more than a bit player. And my main suspect to have killed him was McCaskill. Clearly, as an FBI informant, McCaskill was not murdering anybody in service of Jeffrey.

But whatever my feelings about it, I am better off focusing on the Donnelly side in the trial. The jury will find it much easier to understand the organized-crime, drug culture than the vague militia, dark-web one. If I'm going to emphasize one side as the potential alternative killer to Matt, Donnelly et al. is the way to go.

Hovering over everything is the DNA matched to Matt at the scene. Even if I were able to convince the jury that either Donnelly or Jeffrey or whoever was behind the killing, that doesn't mean that Matt wasn't a part of it.

Steinkamp will be only too happy to point that out.

I do something that I should have done a while ago, something that might ultimately help me out in court. I place a call to Dustin Oliver of the Maine State Police. It's a bit awkward, since he is about to testify for Steinkamp at trial.

"You know I can't talk to you," he says, as soon as he gets on the phone.

"It's not about your testimony, or the case. Well, actually I hope it will be about the case, but only indirectly."

"What the hell are you talking about?"

"I'm calling to make you a hero."

"Then I'm listening."

"There's a place called the Maine Lighthouse brewery; in Warren. They make craft beer; it's owned by Mike Mitchell, former friend and employer of Peter Charkin."

"I thought you said it wasn't about your case?"

"Hear me out. I have reason to believe that they are involved in the drug business with Jerry Donnelly. They may even be manufacturing opioids."

I tell Oliver about the truck labeled Castle Farm Products, a company that does not exist. I say that it makes suspicious deliveries and pickups, then say that I will tell him the opportune time to intercept the truck.

"I need probable cause," he says. "I can't just stop a truck and search it. The fact that it has a fake company name on the side is not illegal. Defense attorneys like you would have me for lunch."

"It also has fake license plates."

"Now you're talking."

We leave it that I will call him when the time is right, and he gives me his cell phone number. In my business that's a sign of some trust.

"The next time we talk will either be on your cell, or in court," I say.

Matt . . . the defendant . . . and I dated for about a year and a half," Carole Peterson says.

"Did you talk about marriage?" Steinkamp asks.

It prompts a smile from Peterson. "We didn't actually talk about it, but we both implied it a lot." Another smile. "We did a lot of implying. But I think we both assumed that's where we'd wind up."

"Is that where you wound up?"

"No. It isn't. We broke up a little more than two years ago."

"Who broke off the relationship?"

"I did."

"I understand these questions are personal," Steinkamp says, displaying fake concern. "But please tell the jury why you did that."

"Well, I guess the easy thing to say is that we grew apart, and I'm sure there was fault on both sides, but Matt changed. He had always been fun and upbeat, but he lost that."

"Did you talk about what was going on?"

"I knew what was going on. He lost his mother; she raised him by herself and they were really close. Then his friend Carl Blanchard died of cancer. That was really tough on Matt; they were very close, and Matt was with him right until the end."

"So he became depressed?"

She nods. "Yes. Dark. It wasn't the Matt I knew."

"How did he handle the breakup?"

"I don't know; I literally wasn't there. I hope I didn't do the wrong thing. I feel now like I let him down when he needed me."

"Did you know Tina Welker, one of the victims in this case?"

"Yes. Tina was a close friend."

"As you felt your relationship with the defendant deteriorating, did you discuss the situation with Ms. Welker?"

"Yes, I talked about it with a lot of my friends. We rely on each other."

"What did she say?"

"That I should break up with Matt, that the relationship was causing me pain and was not going to survive anyway. She felt I'd be better off ending it before we both suffered more pain."

"Did you tell Matt what she said?"

"I've been thinking about that a lot. I believe that I did. Certainly I told him how my friends felt, and I think I mentioned Tina, because she was the most vocal about it."

"How did he react when you told him how your friends felt?"

"He got angry and said it was none of their business. I regretted telling him what they said; I shouldn't have done that. But I was looking for support, for evidence that I was doing the right thing, and that's why I told him."

My first question for Peterson is "When you told Mr. Jantzen that the relationship was over, did he get angry?"

"Yes, he did."

"And you testified that when you told him what your friends said, that he also was angry about that, is that correct?"

She nods. "Yes."

"When he was angry like that, did he hit you?"

"No, of course not."

"Did he threaten you?"

"No."

"Did he try and shoot you?"

"No."

"Were you afraid he was going to physically hurt you?"

"No."

"Why not?"

"Because Matt wasn't like that; he just wasn't violent in that way."

I could leave it there, it's a pretty perfect ending to her testimony, but I decide to go just a bit further. Ms. Peterson seems pleased to be able to say things beneficial to Matt.

"Did you ever see Mr. Jantzen get into a fight? Hit anyone?"

"No."

"Did you ever see him with a gun?"

"No, I did not."

"Did you ever have the thought that maybe you should warn Tina Welker or some of your other friends because Mr. Jantzen was mad at them?"

"No. It never entered my mind."

"Is that because you did not consider him to be a violent person?"

"That's correct."

"Thank you."

Unfortunately, the next time I will talk to Captain Dustin Oliver will be in court, not on his cell phone.

I know that because Steinkamp has just called him to the stand.

The truck that Sam planted the surveillance devices in has not moved, so I couldn't call Oliver to tell him to intercept and board it. I'm beginning to doubt whether it will ever move; it may have been taken out of service.

Ironically, whereas the homicide detective in charge of the case is usually a crucial witness, in this situation that's not true. That's because although he was in charge, he didn't solve the case. He had failed to do so, until the DNA changed everything.

Steinkamp has Oliver briefly describe his career, the commendations he has won, and his recent promotion from lieutenant to captain. It's impressive, and he comes across well to the jury.

In answer to a question, Oliver says, "We took nothing for granted. We considered that Ms. Welker might have been a target, as well as Mr. Charkin. We also considered the very real possibility that it was a random home invasion robbery, which is what it appeared to be."

"What is your theory about what took place in that house?"

"The assailant came in, either allowed in because he knew the occupants, or perhaps through a window. There was one open on the side of the house.

"There was a struggle, probably a brief one, during which Mr. Charkin was punched in the face. He clearly responded and punched or scratched back, because some of the assailant's blood was found on his right hand.

"It's likely that they were then tied to chairs and shot in the head. Of course, we can't be sure of the order of things. They might have been tied up, then Mr. Charkin could have broken free and the struggle ensued then."

"Did those particulars matter to your investigation?"

"Not materially."

"Please describe the progress you made in the investigation."

"I'm afraid that won't take very long. We followed many possibilities, but always ran into the fact that anyone that might qualify as a suspect did not match the DNA on Mr. Charkin's hand. It effectively eliminated them, and frankly, we were stymied."

"But then you caught a break?"

Oliver nods. "We did. We have people that periodically check the DNA submitted to these ancestry sites. Those people have the option to make their submissions public, and there have been cases where we have been able to connect the DNA to a sibling, or to a crime they have themselves committed."

"And that's what happened in this case when Mr. Jantzen submitted his sample?"

"Yes. We traced him to his sister, and then he was found in New Jersey and extradited here."

Oliver has not done us any damage; he didn't have to. But there isn't that much for me to clean up.

"Captain, in your investigation, did you discover that Mr. Charkin was an abuser of opioids?"

"Yes."

"Is that an area you explored, because of your knowledge that drug dealing is often done by violent people?"

"Yes."

"Did you learn who supplied Mr. Charkin with the drugs?"

"We did not."

"But you interviewed many friends and associates of both Ms. Welker and Mr. Charkin?"

"Yes."

"Including Carole Peterson, who was a friend of Ms. Welker and who had recently broken up with Mr. Jantzen?"

"Yes."

"And in all this investigation, and in all these interviews, did the name of Mr. Jantzen ever come up?"

"Not to my knowledge, no."

"Nobody said, 'Hey, this guy is acting strange and is depressed and could be dangerous'?"

"No."

"Did you ever consider the fact that the blood on Mr. Charkin's hand might have been planted, in an effort to absolve the real killer?"

"No, there was nothing to indicate that."

"So it's not possible?"

"Anything is possible; it's not a reasonable hypothesis."

"Doesn't make sense?"

"Correct."

"Let me ask you about some other things, and you can tell me whether they make sense."

"Does it make sense that a killer would follow news accounts of the investigation?"

"I would say so, yes."

"Does it make sense that a killer, knowing from news reports that he left DNA on the scene, would voluntarily make his DNA publicly available?"

"It makes no sense, but murderers don't always behave logically."

"Does it make sense that shortly after making the DNA public, he would return after two years to the area in which the crime took place?"

"Sometimes people act arrogantly, as if they are above the law."

"I asked you if it made sense."

"Not to me."

I let Oliver off the stand, subject to recall by the defense, and we adjourn for lunch. Sam has left a message on my cell phone to call him right away.

"The truck is on the move," he says.

"Tell me everything you know."

"Okay. You're going to love it."

I t's your good friend Andy Carpenter."

Captain Oliver moans. "I think I've had enough of you for today."

"The truck is on the move."

His tone changes immediately. "Talk to me."

"It should be at the brewery in two hours; it will be coming down the 295. According to my sources, it is carrying three cases of thebaine."

Oliver whistles softly. He obviously knows that thebaine is a key ingredient in making synthetic opioids. It is itself an opiate alkaloid, chemically similar to codeine and morphine. "You're sure of this?"

"Positive. The truck is filled with boxes of stuff to make beer. The three boxes of thebaine are in the middle of them; if you bring a canine drug detector, the dog will find it in a minute." I don't mention that Simon Garfunkel could easily do the trick. Oliver will have other dogs to help if he wants them.

"You have an idea how we should proceed?"

"Funny you should ask. I think you should stop the truck for the improper license plate, then search the vehicle. The dog can give you even more probable cause. Once you've found the thebaine, you can head for the brewery. The fact that the thebaine was headed there gives you all the probable cause you need to enter.

"Once you're in there, there are two very large rooms, each one like a warehouse. One is where they produce the beer; I suspect the other is where they manufacture the drugs."

"How do we know the truck is headed there?"

"Ask the driver before you let him know you're going to search the truck. He would have no reason to withhold it. You also might find a GPS with the brewery address in it, or a work order. You're an investigator; figure it out."

"How do you know all this?"

"That is not something I am going to share with you."

"What a surprise. The people who work for me think you're full of shit and this is going to blow up in our face."

"Then you need to work on your hiring criteria. Please call me later to let me know how it went. You can also thank me then and apologize for doubting me."

Click.

While Captain Oliver is off doing whatever he's doing, the main event is about to unfold in the courtroom.

Steinkamp's witness is Sergeant Sarah Gentry, who works in forensics. Charlie Tilton has warned me that she makes an excellent witness; she is widely respected and fully understands her craft, though apparently she can be a contentious witness under cross-examination.

I hate people like that, except for the contentious part. That always works in my favor.

Steinkamp gets the uncomfortable part out of the way first. He gets Gentry to say that she did not actually work this case two years ago, that Sergeant Anthony Rojas was in charge. Unfortunately for Steinkamp, and certainly for Rojas, he passed away last year.

"You have access to all of Sergeant Rojas's notes and records from the case?" Steinkamp asks.

"Yes."

"And you've studied them?"

"Yes, of course. Thoroughly."

"Let's focus on the blood found on Mr. Charkin's hands. Was it possible to retrieve DNA from that?"

"Yes."

"There was a great deal of blood from the gunshot wound that Mr. Charkin suffered. Did that not mix with the blood on his hand?"

"It did not."

"So the sample was pure?"

"Pure, but slightly degraded. That is not uncommon in cases like this and can be due to a variety of factors. We use a technique called PCR to make sure we get an accurate reading."

Steinkamp takes twenty minutes having her explain the intricacies of PCR testing. The jurors, even though they must understand that this is the key testimony, look like they might doze off. I wouldn't mind a sleeper couch myself.

That turns out not to be the most boring part. After she describes how there were no matches for the DNA in any of the federal or state systems, she gets to the sample that Matt sent to the ancestry site.

She goes into a lengthy discourse on the individual markers in the DNA strands that prove that the two samples match and says that the chance it is wrong is less than one in a quadrillion. I've lost bets on football games with odds better than that, but I don't think I'll point that out on cross-examination.

The entire process takes until three thirty, and Judge Pressley asks if I'd like to start my questioning now or hold off until tomorrow. Even though I'm anxious to hear from Captain Oliver, I want to score whatever points I can rather than let the jury spend the night thinking Gentry's testimony is unchallenged.

Her body language changes as I approach. She stiffens, as if gearing up for the battle. I'm fine with that. "Sergeant Gentry, you said that the DNA sample was degraded, and—"

She interrupts me, not trying to conceal her annoyance. "I said 'slightly degraded.'"

"Right. This might go faster if you let me ask the question, then you can include your corrections, or 'slight' corrections, in your answer. What can cause DNA degradation?"

"A variety of factors. Temperature, time, ultraviolent light, radiation . . ."

"Do you know what the temperature was the night of the murders?"

She shakes her head, shrugging off the question. "It doesn't matter."

"Have you ever testified in court before?"

She smiles her condescension. "Many times."

"Then I would have thought that by now you would know that your role as a witness is not to determine what questions matter; it's to answer them."

Steinkamp objects, but Pressley overrules and instructs Gentry to answer the questions she is asked.

"I do not know the temperature from that day," she says.

I submit a US Weather printout showing a heat wave at that time; it was eighty-seven degrees that night. That is hot for Maine. "Is that the kind of temperature that can degrade DNA?"

"It's possible, depending on exposure."

I point out that in Sergeant Rojas's notes, it was four hours from the time the DNA was collected to the time it was checked into the lab. Rojas had two other calls to make before he got back there to enter it.

Gentry counters that it doesn't matter, that the truck is refrigerated and always locked.

"Really?" I feign surprise. "You were there and saw that it was refrigerated and locked?"

"It always is."

"Were you there?"

"No."

"Sergeant Gentry, you said that the blood DNA matched Mr. Jantzen. What about the skin?"

"What do you mean?" She pretends to be frustrated by my question.

"I assume they found traces of skin that did not belong to either of the victims?"

"It's not in the report."

"Correct me if I'm wrong, because I'm not a doctor. But isn't the blood under the skin?"

"Obviously."

"So for the blood to come out and go on Mr. Charkin's hand, wouldn't skin have to break first? Isn't that sort of a medical principle?"

"There were no traces of skin found in the report. Sergeant Rojas was very precise."

"Did you not understand the question? I asked if the skin would have to break for blood to come out."

"Of course it would. But no skin was found."

"Not on the victim's fist, maybe under the nails?"

She gives an exaggerated frown to make sure the jury knows she's annoyed. "None was found."

We go back and forth on stuff like this for another twenty minutes. I'm not making great progress, just trying to put doubt in the jurors' minds. I'll have more to say about this in the defense case.

Steinkamp rehabilitates her a bit on a redirect, but there's not much work for him to do.

Then he says the words that I simultaneously look forward to and dread.

"The state rests."

While we are waiting for Captain Oliver to call and tell me what happened, Laurie and I find out what happened another way: we watch television.

It's a huge, developing story on all newscasts: A drug raid was executed on the Maine Lighthouse brewery in Warren, uncovering three-quarters of a million dollars' worth of synthetic opioids. Even more significant is that the site was being used to produce the stuff.

Captain Oliver of the Maine State Police, the guy who hasn't bothered to call me, holds a press conference with other state cops behind him, as well as a representative from the FBI and one from the ATF. When credit is up for grabs, these people can assemble quickly.

Oliver hides behind the old standby "We cannot comment on an ongoing investigation," but he confirms that the drugs and the manufacturing setup was uncovered, as well as trace explosives in the brewery and in a truck that carried the contraband, though no explosives were actually found in either place.

He says that the owner of the brewery, Michael Mitchell, has been taken into custody, along with three other employees. Oliver also credits a K-9 team as helping in the investigation. He thanks the FBI and the ATF for their cooperation, although for the life of me I have no idea what they had to do with anything.

Noticeably absent from his thankfulness is any mention of Andy Carpenter, attorney-at-law, who made the entire goddamn thing happen. Nor does he comment on the fact that murder victim Peter Charkin was an employee at the company, and an associate of Michael Mitchell's.

"Well, you brought down a drug ring," Laurie says.

"Yeah, it will give Matt Jantzen something to tell his fellow inmates for the next forty years."

"So you're not pleased about this? It's not good news?"

"It's good news, but it's a low bar. I'm glad Mitchell is going down, and maybe they'll even get Donnelly, though I doubt it. In terms of our case, it adds some more smoke to a defense that is all smoke and mirrors."

"What does it add?"

"Now when I talk about Charkin being involved with bad guys, the jury doesn't have to take my word for it. I have proof."

"But no proof that the bad guys killed him."

I nod. "There is that. Also no idea how they managed to plant Matt Jantzen's blood on the scene."

The phone rings and Laurie picks it up. After a few moments, she hands it to me. "Captain Oliver."

I pick up the phone. "You cracked the case."

"Another example of the value of diligent police work."

"I look forward to your testifying as part of the defense case."

"You can't be serious," he says, the sarcasm gone from his voice. "I've got nothing to help you . . . no connection to Charkin's death to point to."

"In the hands of a lesser attorney, that might be significant." Then, "Charkin was right in the middle of a major drug manufacturing and dealing operation."

"Maybe so; I don't know whether he was a significant player or not. But I have no information as to why they would have killed him."

This is depressing, so I switch subjects. "How about Donnelly? Will you be able to nail him?"

"Not sure yet. We have to sift through all the evidence, all the records that we confiscated. I've got a feeling that our best shot will be to get Mitchell to finger him in a plea deal."

"I doubt he'll do it. Mitchell will know that Donnelly has people that can get to him in prison."

"You might be right, but we'll certainly put the pressure on. Mitchell is facing a lot of years."

"He deserves it, but not as much as Donnelly."

"Look on the bright side: this is going to put a huge crimp in Donnelly's operation. He was in financial trouble before, and this had to have been his major income source."

"Maybe we should run a benefit for him."

"Cheer up," Oliver says. "Today was a good day."

"Yeah? You wouldn't think so if you spent it at the defense table."

"If I find anything that helps you, I'll make sure you know about it."

"Thanks. See you in court."

The most important decision in most trials is an easy one in this case.

I'm referring to the determination of whether a defendant should testify on his own behalf. To the uninitiated, it would seem that the answer should most often be yes. After all, who better to protest his or her innocence than the person claiming to be innocent? And wouldn't the lack of testimony be seen as a tacit admission of guilt?

The real-life answer to the question of whether to testify is almost always no. There's just too much risk in having the client face what is certainly going to be a withering cross-examination. Any mistake, and even innocent people can make mistakes, especially under tremendous pressure, would be fatal.

Usually it's a balance of risk versus reward, but in this case there is almost no reward. Matt's position, and mine, is that he has absolutely no information to offer about the killings. All he can do is say that he wasn't involved, not exactly an earthshaking comment for an accused individual. It defines self-serving.

Matt cannot even say where he was on the night in question. This could look suspicious and certainly wouldn't be helpful, even though probably all the members of the jury have no idea where they were that night either.

Before court this morning, I discussed the situation with Matt, and he agreed with my assessment that he not testify. He professed to have full faith in me, which will make it even more painful when the jury comes back with the inevitable guilty verdict.

Matt is looking hopeful this morning, with the start of the defense case imminent. Charlie Tilton doesn't seem to share that view, basically since Charlie has a more accurate assessment of our chances.

We're starting off slowly, with Mary Patrick, Matt's half sister.

"Please describe your relationship to Mr. Jantzen."

"I'm his half sister. We have the same father, but different mothers."

"So you didn't grow up together?"

"No. I not only never spoke to Matt until a few months ago, but we didn't even know that each other existed."

"How did you come to meet?"

"Well, I had sent my DNA in more than two years ago, to origin.com. I wanted to learn things about my ancestry, although I never thought I might have siblings. It turns out that Matt did the same thing a few months ago, and they told him about me."

"When you sign up for one of those things, you have to agree that they can share the information with the public, and with governmental agencies like law enforcement?"

"That's correct. Both Matt and I did that."

"So he contacted you?"

"Yes. He called me and said"—she smiles broadly—"'I'm your brother.' I was shocked, as you can imagine."

"What happened next?"

"Well, I said I'd love to meet him, and he told me that he

had already decided to move back to Maine. He grew up here. Next thing I knew, there he was. We hit it off really well immediately."

"Did he ever mention the murders?"

"No, never."

"Did he ever seem worried, or guarded, about anything? I'm looking for your impression."

"No, never."

I have her describe how she came to realize that Matt might be in trouble; it's an area of concern for our defense. A suspect who runs can be said to show consciousness of guilt.

The police had come to her when she first handed her DNA in and came back when Matt's was recorded. She told him about it, and he took off for New Jersey.

"I told him to leave to take time to think about what to do," she says. "He was shocked and confused, but he agreed."

Steinkamp's cross-examination is brief but effective. "So, Ms. Patrick, you spent a total of two weeks knowing Mr. Jantzen before he left Maine?"

"That's correct."

"So all your impressions of him come from that brief period?"

"Yes."

"When you told him about your concerns that the police might be after him, he fled the state?"

"He followed my advice to take time to study the situation and think about how best to handle it."

"He went to New Jersey to study?"

"To consider his options."

"After he fled this state?"

"He needed to be away from here. That's what he said, and that's what I said."

Steinkamp nods, as if that clears it up. "Right, let's talk about what he said, or didn't say. Did he say that he needed to clear this up by going to the police and correcting their error?"

"No."

"Did he say that he was elsewhere at the time of the murders, and that once he demonstrates that, everything will be fine?"

"No. He barely remembered the murders and didn't know where he was that night."

"Did you remember the murders?"

"Yes."

"Because it was a big story back then, correct?"

"It was a story. I remembered it more clearly because of the visit I had from the police."

"Ms. Patrick, I think we all understand that you want to protect your brother, but you know very little about him. Isn't that true?"

"I believe in him."

"Because he's family." It's a statement, not a question.

Mary Patrick nods and replies in a soft voice, "Because he's family."

Officer John Pataki of the Paterson Police Department defines "reluctant witness."

He certainly could not have realized that breaking up a fight on Park Avenue in Paterson, New Jersey, would cause him to be in Maine testifying in a murder trial.

And he certainly did not want to be here. We had to subpoena him, always a dangerous thing to do with a witness that we hope to be favorable. But after he got here, Laurie put him into still another suite, fed him lobster rolls, and convinced him it was for a good cause.

I don't know how friendly a witness he will be, but I do know he loves lobster.

After I get him to identify himself as a Paterson police officer, I ask, "Lieutenant, you were called to the corner of Park Avenue and Thirty-third Street?"

"Yes, someone had placed a nine-one-one call that there was a fight going on."

"What did you find when you arrived?"

"The fight was over. One of the participants, a Mr. Neal Keller, was on the ground. He was dazed and making no effort to get up. The other participant, Matthew Jantzen, was standing near him, holding a dog on a leash."

"Were there a number of bystanders nearby who claimed to be witnesses to the event?"

"Yes, we questioned seven people, all of whom told the same story."

"Was I one of those people?"

"Yes."

"And my wife, Laurie Collins, was another?"

"Yes."

"And what was the story we all told?"

"That Mr. Keller was abusing his dog. He was kicking him and yelling at him to get up. Mr. Jantzen ran over and yelled at him to stop. Mr. Keller attacked him, and Mr. Jantzen defended himself and quickly prevailed in the fight."

"So he got in this fight, understanding that it might well bring the police, because he wanted to help a dog?"

"I can't speak to what he understood, but he was definitely acting to prevent the dog from being hurt."

"When he saw you arrive, did he try to run?"

"No."

"When you said you were taking both men into custody, did he resist?"

"No."

"Try to talk you out of it?"

"No."

"Thank you, no further questions."

Steinkamp stands, using my fake put-upon frown, as if he is annoyed he has to deal with these trivialities. I might add that compared to me he's a fake-frown amateur.

"Officer Pataki, when you arrived, the fight had already ended?"

"Yes."

"It was a violent fight?"

"That's what the witnesses said."

"And according to those witnesses, Mr. Jantzen punched Mr. Keller into submission? Near unconsciousness?"

"Yes."

"Based on your investigation, Mr. Jantzen did not know Mr. Keller before he pummeled him?"

"He did not know him, but the witnesses reported that Mr. Keller threw the first punch."

"Did those witnesses describe Mr. Jantzen as someone who had likely never been in a fight before?"

"They didn't comment on it either way."

"But Mr. Jantzen was the clear winner?"

"Yes. That much is certain."

"Thank you."

I didn't get that much out of Officer Pataki; certainly nothing that will carry the day. But at the least, he got across the point that Jantzen was willing to risk a great deal to rescue a dog that was being abused.

If any dog lovers are on the jury, and in Maine there have to be, then that was worth the price of a suite and a few lobster rolls.

've made a decision; I made it the other night while walking the dogs.

I'm next going to present evidence of Charkin's being in bed with bad people, then wrap it up with my feeble attack on the DNA evidence.

I'm doing it that way, in that order, because I want the jury to know that there were other potential killers of Charkin. They might then view my attacks on the DNA evidence in a more sympathetic light.

To that end I'm meeting Captain Oliver in an anteroom an hour before court starts, so that we can go over his testimony. There's no way I can tell him what to say, but I do want him prepared for my questions. He's not happy to be back here, so I've brought him a few muffins from the hotel as a peace offering.

"These are good," he says, his mouth full.

"There's more where those came from, depending on your performance today."

He nods and reaches for another muffin. "Think of this as a successful bribe."

I briefly take him through what I will ask about Mitchell and the drug situation. He says that he might decline to answer a few of the questions because of the ongoing investigation, which is fine with me.

Then I mention McCaskill, and I get a surprising reaction.

"I can't go there. My chief got a call from the FBI."

"Saying what?"

"That it would interfere with an investigation, and that McCaskill and the militia connection are off-limits."

"Was this Agent Nichols?"

"No, I know Don Nichols; he would have called me directly. This came from much higher up."

"Why would they tie McCaskill to your testimony in this case?"

"I can't answer that; I don't know. Maybe because Charkin was somehow involved with him."

"I can't prove that. I wasn't even sure I was going to ask you about McCaskill. What do you know that would tie him to Charkin?"

Oliver shrugs. "Not much. I had evidence they knew each other, but nothing more than that."

"Did you know he was an FBI informant?"

Oliver does a double take. "No. Are you sure about that?"

"I am. What the hell could the FBI be afraid of? Why would they think McCaskill was connected to this trial? Why would they try and preemptively muzzle you when you had nothing to say in the first place?"

Oliver can't answer those questions, and I sure can't, so I give up and we head into court. Steinkamp looks surprised to see Oliver; I doubt Steinkamp expected me to recall the cop that arrested Matt.

"Captain Oliver, an event took place the other night at the Maine Lighthouse brewery. Can you describe for the jury what happened?"

I imagine that most if not all of the jurors are familiar with it, since it was big news here.

Oliver describes the raid, emphasizing the substantial nature of the drug operation that was taken down.

"Did Peter Charkin work for the Maine Lighthouse brewery?" I ask.

"Yes, until not long before his death."

"And there was testimony earlier that the toxicological report on Charkin showed a substantial level of opioids in his system?"

"That's correct."

"Were they synthetic? The same type as manufactured at the Maine Lighthouse brewery?"

"Yes."

"There was also evidence that Charkin had been receiving cash in large increments, and had five thousand in cash in his apartment when he died. Is that correct?"

"Yes."

"Did he have a job at that time?"

"No, he had already left the company."

"Do you know the circumstances under which he left?"

"That is unclear."

"Could he have had a falling out with his employer?"

"Certainly possible."

"Over drugs?"

"I couldn't say."

"Could he possibly have been blackmailing them, threatening to expose their operation?"

Steinkamp objects that it is speculation, and Pressley sustains. That's fine; I've planted the possibility in the jurors' minds.

"Is there an organized crime connection to this case? Were the drugs being distributed as part of a larger criminal conspiracy?"

"That is under investigation, so I can't get into details. But there certainly is such a connection."

"Are these people, in your view, capable of murder?"

"No question about it."

"Are you familiar with the name Henry Stokan?"

"Yes. Mr. Stokan was an enforcer who did some work for that criminal organization."

"A hit man?"

"I prefer the term *enforcer*," Oliver says.

"Was there a connection between Mr. Charkin and Mr. Stokan?"

"Yes, though in our original investigation we were not able to determine the significance."

"Is Mr. Stokan here today?"

"No, Mr. Stokan was recently murdered. His body was found in the river with a bullet in his head."

"So in your original investigation you were able to connect Mr. Charkin to a number of very dangerous people?"

"Yes, that's safe to say."

"Was Mr. Jantzen one of them?"

"No."

"Thank you."

Steinkamp starts by saying, "That's quite a story, Captain. Congratulations on your successful operation the other night."

"Thank you."

"You mentioned some dangerous people, and you alluded to others. Do you have any evidence at all that one of those people killed Tina Welker and Peter Charkin?"

"No."

"Not a shred?"

"We have no such evidence."

"Did any of these evil people leave their blood and DNA at the murder scene?"

"No."

"You said that there is an organized crime connection, is that correct?"

"Yes."

"In your experience, when hired hit men kill someone on behalf of organized crime, do they take pains to make it look like a home invasion?"

"Not in my experience."

"Do they generally frame someone else with forensic evidence?"

"Not in my experience."

"Of course not. Their victims are, like Mr. Stokan, found in the river with a bullet in their heads. No further questions."

I am not going to question our DNA expert.

I spoke to her briefly the other night on the phone, and that was enough for me to make my decision. Charlie Tilton knows this stuff much better than me, and he's willing to do it, so I'm going to let him.

It's basically an act of self-preservation. The subject matter is so dry, and the likelihood of anything being said to sway the jury is so small, that my brain would explode if I had to participate.

And like I said, Charlie will do a better job.

So I'll half listen to the testimony with my unexploded brain, since I know what each of them are going to say. With the other half of my brain I'll take the time to agonize about the many things that are bugging me. It feels like a puzzle with pieces missing, and the ones I have don't seem to fit.

Our expert is Ruth Kennedy, a criminology professor at Boston University, who makes a nice living doubling as an expert witness, with a specialty in forensics.

Charlie takes her through her curriculum vitae, which I am sure would be impressive if I were listening.

The FBI being concerned about this case is bugging me. They are involved in the militia side of things, and I have obviously helped them in that regard. But why would they be worried about Captain Oliver's potential testimony about Charkin and Mitchell and Donnelly and the drug side of Charkin's life?

"So the DNA in this case was partially degraded?" Charlie asks.

Kennedy nods. "No question about it. That's why PCR was necessary to get a type."

The name that has started to emerge from the deep recesses of my mind is Henry Stokan. Stokan was stalking me for no particularly good reason. He wasn't going to scare me off, and he didn't make an attempt to kill me.

Killing me, or even beating me up, would have been illogical and counterproductive. It would have drawn more attention to Jerry Donnelly, and a person with Donnelly's experience in matters of this kind would have known better.

"Could the high temperature that day have caused the degradation?" Charlie asks.

"Certainly, if the sample was exposed to it for any length of time. There is no way to determine that either way from the notes, and Sergeant Rojas is unfortunately not here to explain his actions."

When Marcus dealt with Stokan that night, Stokan gave up Donnelly's name easily. That's another strange thing: Why would he do that? There was certainly a chance he could end up in the river. In fact, he did.

He also said that Charkin did not get drugs from Donnelly or his lieutenant/dealer Carmody. Why say that? Why make something like that up if it wasn't true? How would lying about that help Stokan?

It wouldn't.

"What about the lengthy period of time that it took between

the sample being taken from the victim's hand and when it was checked into the lab?"

Kennedy nods. "Again, it all depends on what happened during that period of time. But I assure you, a delay like that runs counter to accepted procedures, here and everywhere."

We know that Stokan had done some enforcer work for Donnelly, but in trying to scare or hurt me, could he have been working for someone else?

And where did Charkin fit into all of this? Was he a bit player, on the fringe of these criminal worlds? Or was he somehow at or near the center?

"Have you studied the storage procedures that were used in the van and at the lab?"

"Yes, and there is a great deal that concerns me."

Furthermore, I do not understand why McCaskill was killed. If he was an FBI informant who had turned on the FBI and was working for Darrin Jeffrey and the militia, why would they have killed him?

"What are some other ways that blood DNA could become degraded in the way it was in this case?"

"Besides temperature and a long period of time, certainly ultraviolet light could do it, or simple irradiation."

Charlie responds with another question, but I don't hear it. I need to get out of this courtroom.

But I can't, at least, not right now.

I tell Charlie during the afternoon break that he needs to use up the rest of the day questioning the witness.

"Are you nuts? I ran out of material ten minutes ago. The jurors are so bored they have a bridge game going."

"I don't care what you say, but we can't adjourn our case today. Tell the judge we'll have more witnesses on Monday. I need the weekend."

"What's going on?"

"I'll tell you later. Meanwhile, I've got to get out of here."

"You're leaving?"

"Yes. Can't be helped. If the judge asks what's going on, tell her that I have full confidence in you. No, she'll never believe that. Tell her I'm not feeling well."

"Wiseass."

I look at my watch and see that only five minutes remain until the end of the break. I want to be out of here by then, but first I have to talk to my client, who is still sitting at the defense table.

"Matt, something's come up. We only have a few minutes."

"What is it?"

"You told me that when you left Maine originally, it was because things were not going well. You said you had a friend who died of cancer."

"Right. Carl Blanchard."

"Right. We need to talk about Carl Blanchard."

My first call is to Laurie to run it by her, to give her a chance to tell me I'm nuts.

She doesn't; I can tell by the excitement in her voice that she thinks I'm right. I'm heading for the hotel, so I ask her to get the team together for a meeting in our room in a couple of hours.

I have two important calls to make to enlist help for what I need. The first one is to Ginny Lawson, Tina Welker's friend and coworker at the hospital.

I get a message that the department is closed until Monday, so I try her on the cell phone number she gave me. "Ginny, I have a big favor to ask you."

"What is it?" She sounds wary, which is not surprising. I am, after all, still representing the person she thinks killed her friend.

"I need you to go to your office at the hospital."

"It's closed. They've been renovating each weekend and they're turning over the machines tomorrow night."

"What exactly does 'turning over the machines' mean?"

"Replacing the cesium cores."

"Even though the office is closed, can you get in to retrieve something? It will just take a few minutes."

"What do you need?"

I tell her, but it doesn't reduce her skepticism. "What will that accomplish?"

"I believe it will help me prove who actually killed your friend."

There's a pause. "Okay. I'm on my way."

"Thank you. Can you email it to me?"

She promises to do that, so I give her my email address.

One down, one big one to go.

My next call is to Captain Oliver, who groans when he hears that it's me. It's a reaction I have heard many times in my life.

"What is it this time?"

"I'm sorry, but is this the guy I turned into a state hero? The guy who because of me will likely be promoted to a position way above his level of competence?"

"You called to insult me? I testified for you. What do you want me to do now, arrest the members of the jury before they can deliberate?"

"What I am about to do for you will make the raid at the brewery feel like just another day at the office."

"I'm listening." The change in tone in his voice is clear. I delivered for him the first time, so I have legal street cred.

"But there are things you have to do for me."

"Uh-oh."

"And the whole thing has to be done on my terms; I am calling the shots. Otherwise I turn it over to the FBI, and they get the glory."

"You going to get to the point anytime soon?"

"My terms?"

A beat, and then, "Unless you're asking me to do something illegal."

"I'm not. If you have any weekend plans, cancel them."

Bail was set at $2 million in the Mike Mitchell case, which is why he is currently sitting in county jail.

According to Charlie Tilton, Mitchell is arranging for the money to be posted, but it takes time because the value of some houses and property he owns has to be assigned. That is expected to be accomplished on Monday, but since this is only Saturday, he's still sitting there, exactly where I want him.

When I arrive at the jail, the director is waiting for me. "Good morning, Mr. Carpenter. We've been expecting you."

"I assume you spoke to Captain Oliver?"

"At length."

"And you've set up the interview?"

"I have. It's quite unusual for Mitchell not to have the option of having his lawyer present."

"He can refuse to talk to me or ask for the lawyer."

"Very well. Mr. Mitchell will be brought into the interview room momentarily."

"Does he know he'll be talking to me?"

"I don't believe so, no. Was he supposed to be so informed?"

"Doesn't matter; he'll find out soon enough."

The director brings me into an interview room, and a guard

brings Mitchell in a few minutes later. He is handcuffed and in prison garb; this is a guy who has experienced a fall from grace.

"Shit. What do you want?" Then, "Actually, it doesn't matter. I don't want to talk to you."

"You think you don't, but you do. Because I'm here to make your situation better. Not great, but much better."

This seems to get his attention. "You've got five minutes."

I shake my head. "You're the one running out of time. And you've got one chance; don't blow it. Right now you're charged with a major drug offense. It's a big deal, but it's not mass murder. So you can be on the right side of this, or the wrong side. Because I know everything."

I'm lying about this. What I have are suspicions. Strong ones, but suspicions. I need Mitchell to confirm it all.

"You don't know anything."

"Really? Let's start with this. I know that Tina Welker was the target that night."

I watch his facial expressions and body language go from surprise, to surrender, to trying to figure out the best course for himself.

Finally he nods. "Okay, I'm listening."

"No, Mitchell. I'm the one listening. You need to start talking. You testify to what you know, and I can promise you that Captain Oliver will go to bat for you. You'll plead it out, serve a few years, and spend the rest of your life sampling craft beer.

"You keep quiet and you'll go down as a mass murderer. Either way we're breaking this up, and your partners will sell you out in a heartbeat."

He thinks about it. "Okay."

"How did Tina Welker get involved?"

"Charkin brought her in. She needed money; her mother was sick."

"What did she do?"

"She told Charkin the layout at the hospital; where all the machines were. They were supposed to be changed out, something about the cores being made with cesium. It's radioactive stuff."

"This was for the militia group? Darrin Jeffrey?"

"Yes, they did everything. But they got to Jerry Donnelly through Charkin . . . offered him big money to be a part of it."

"What was Charkin's role?"

"He was at the center of it all. He knew Donnelly because of the drug operation; we were making the stuff for him. And he knew the militia guys through McCaskill. He brought everyone together."

"So why was he killed?"

"That wasn't us; that was the militia guys. They're crazy. They want to start a civil war."

"That doesn't answer my question. Why was Charkin killed?"

"That wasn't supposed to happen. Jeffrey got Henry Stokan to handle it; Donnelly supplied him. He was supposed to kill Welker that night, but Charkin was there. Stokan didn't even know him, so he figured he couldn't leave a witness when he killed Tina."

"Why did they want to kill her?"

"She stole the blood . . . Jantzen's blood. She did it because Charkin asked her to; she didn't know why. She didn't realize she was using it to frame someone for her own murder.

"But they killed her because she figured out why they wanted to know about the machines and the cesium, that they were going to make bombs. It freaked her out. She talked to Charkin about going to the FBI, and he ratted her out. He knew that if she went to the FBI, he'd go down with everybody else."

"Did Donnelly know the militia's plan?"

"You mean about the bombs? I guess he must have, but I

didn't. At least, I didn't know about the radioactive stuff. Not until it was too late to do anything about it. I swear."

"Why did Donnelly go along with all this?"

"Are you kidding? They paid him huge money. Those guys were loaded; I don't know where they get it."

"Why did she steal Matt Jantzen's blood?"

"They checked him out. He had no DNA on file anywhere, no military, no police record, nothing. They didn't want him to get caught, they just wanted to shift suspicion away from them."

"So my client, Matt Jantzen, did not kill Tina Welker and Peter Charkin?"

"He did not."

"We're going to have this same conversation on Monday, in front of the jury. See you then, Mitchell."

At 3:00 P.M., Corey, Marcus, Laurie, and I arrive at the radiology building of Augusta General Hospital and Medical Center.

Two state police officers accompany us. The building is closed, and the only person present is Carla Levante, the director, who was installed two years ago.

The officers take her into custody, allegedly for questioning, but really to get her out of the way so that she cannot make a phone call and abort what is about to happen.

The building has been under surveillance by Captain Oliver's people for six hours, in case events moved faster than we expected. But my expectation was that it would be done at night, and it seems as if that is the case.

We had a contingency plan in case we were wrong; it would have been slightly less subtle and significantly more violent.

The large truck pulls up at a little after 8:00 P.M. That it is unmarked is as expected; security demands it. The cargo it is carrying is valuable, and in normal times there is no sense tipping off potential thieves and terrorists.

These are not normal times.

From my vantage point I see six men get out. Two are dressed in work clothes. The other four are not. They head for the front door of the building, looking around to confirm that they are not being observed.

They do not realize that at this moment they are among the most observed people on the planet.

They enter the building and one of them, Darrin Jeffrey, looks around to make sure the place is secure. Jeffrey turns and says, "Bring it in." Three of the men, including one dressed in work clothes, who is clearly a prisoner of the other two, go outside.

They won't be back.

That leaves Jeffrey, one of his people, and the other man in work clothes. "Get started," Jeffrey says, and the man in work clothes nods and starts walking to the huge machine at the rear of the room.

"No, don't." The voice is Captain Oliver's. He has come out of hiding, gun in hand, to take over. Marcus and I come out as well. Laurie and Corey are outside, helping officers deal with the other three men.

Jeffrey's partner must not have gotten the memo that they are in a helpless situation, and he reaches for his weapon. It is the last reach he ever makes, as Oliver puts a bullet in his chest.

Jeffrey takes a different tack; he starts to run toward the door. Marcus is just a bit quicker; he catches Jeffrey from behind, grabbing his shirt behind his neck and throwing him to the ground. In football that's called a horse-collar tackle and results in a penalty. The way Marcus employs it, the name is even more apt, because he does it with enough force to literally tackle a horse.

Captain Oliver makes a quick call, and the place immediately looks like a police convention. An ambulance arrives to deal with the guy that Oliver shot, but it quickly becomes clear that he is more in need of a coroner.

It takes a while for everyone to feel completely confident that the area is secure. People from the state energy department have arrived to take possession of the machine in the truck, which was the major reason all of this took place.

I see Darrin Jeffrey sitting handcuffed in a chair, soon to be taken away. I've always loved the end of *A Few Good Men,* when Tom Cruise triumphantly says to Jack Nicholson, "Don't call me son. I'm a lawyer and an officer in the United States Navy. And you're under arrest, you son of a bitch."

It's every lawyer's dream to repeat that scene, and this is my chance. I walk over to Jeffrey; I can see out of the corner of my eye that Laurie is following me to make sure I don't do something I shouldn't.

Jeffrey looks up at me. "What the hell do you want?"

I look him right in the eye. "Don't call me son. I'm a lawyer and an officer in the United States Navy. And you're under arrest, you son of a bitch."

Laurie takes me by the arm and gently pulls me away. "Good job, Admiral."

We resume our waiting, and finally, after almost an hour and a half, Oliver comes over to me. "I have to admit, you do nice work."

I smile. "When you do the press conference, it's *Andy* Carpenter. *Andrew* sounds too formal. I'm a person of the people."

"I'll try and remember."

"Are we done here?"

He nods. "We're done here."

Once again, Captain Oliver conducts a press conference victory lap, and once again he neglects to mention me.

A couple of hours later he calls and I point out that he slighted me again.

"Sorry about that. In all the excitement I forgot which you preferred, *Andy* or *Andrew.* I figured it was best to leave you out entirely rather than make a mistake. I'm sure you understand."

"You're an ungrateful glory hound."

He laughs. "Ah, so you do understand." Then, "How did it go with Mitchell?"

"Could not have been better. He's going to testify on Monday; he agreed, and his lawyer has since advised him it was the right move to make in order to get a favorable sentence."

"So he's going to plead guilty?"

"He really has no choice."

"Then you're feeling good about your chances?"

"Not yet. What happened at the brewery, and yesterday at the hospital, was better news for you than me. None of it speaks to who actually killed Charkin."

"But you'll have Mitchell's testimony."

"When that happens, then I'll feel confident. Or at least I

would, if I ever felt confident about anything." Switching the subject, I ask, "How many dirty bombs would they have been able to make?"

"They would have had the cesium from the new machine core that irradiates the blood, also what was left from the old machine, and from all the individual radiation machines, plus their replacements. The short answer to your question is probably seven or eight bombs; the damage could have been catastrophic."

"Why did they wait so long to do this?"

"Because they were playing the long game. They needed to wait for the hospital to replace the cesium. That stuff lasts a while; the delay must have driven them crazy."

"Where was the first target, do you know? . . . Wait . . . let me guess. Fenway Park."

"Bingo . . . not bad."

"It comes naturally to me. What's going to happen to Darrin Jeffrey?"

"He's going down. He hasn't said a word, but his colleagues are talking nonstop. I think we're going to get Jerry Donnelly as well. But if there's a civil war, Jeffrey is going to have to listen to it on the radio."

We get off the phone and I start to prepare for tomorrow morning. I have not had the chance to prep Mitchell, other than our interview, and he will not be thrilled to be testifying. I want to make sure I force him to cover all the relevant points.

Charlie Tilton comes to the hotel to help in the preparation. We work for a couple of hours, then Laurie comes in with food for dinner.

While we're eating, Charlie says, "I can't believe I almost turned down this job."

"You did turn it down."

"You're holding that against me? Anyway, I'm very glad you talked me into it."

"It's no big deal. This happens every day back in New York."

"New Jersey."

"Whatever."

Charlie's cell phone rings and he seems surprised when he looks at the caller ID. He answers with "Hello" and then just listens. A full minute goes by before he says, "Okay." Then he hangs up.

"That was quite a conversation," I say.

"You have no idea. Mike Mitchell is dead. He was found hanging in his cell."

strongly doubt that Mitchell hanged himself.

I had just presented him with a pathway to a lighter sentence, so doing it at that point made no sense. My suspicion is that Donnelly's people got to him in the jail.

Bottom line is that it doesn't matter. It is a crushing blow to our defense, mainly because the defense attorney is an idiot. I should have taped the conversation in the jail. I could have played it in court; it would have been an obvious exception to the hearsay rule.

I did have my reason for not taping it. I would have been obligated to turn it over to the prosecution as a work product, and had it not gone the way I wanted, it could have hurt us.

But I should have taped it and I didn't, and my client very well may suffer for it.

I call Ginny Lawson to the stand. "Ms. Lawson, you currently work at Augusta General Hospital and Medical Center?"

"Yes, in the radiology department."

"What is done in that department?"

"Well, in addition to taking X-rays, we also do radiation therapy for cancer patients, and we irradiate blood to be used in transfusions."

"Why is the irradiation necessary?"

"It prevents donor white cells from reproducing and attacking within a patient's weakened immune system. I could get more technical if you'd like."

I smile. "Not necessary. . . . We heard testimony earlier in the trial that irradiation can degrade DNA . . . are you familiar with that?"

"I'm sorry. I'm not."

I knew she wasn't; I just wanted the jury to remember it, which is why I put it in the question. I introduce a document into evidence and ask her to describe it.

"It's a record of a blood donation made at Augusta General."

"Does it list the purpose?"

"It was donated in the name of a patient there at the time, one Carl Blanchard."

"How many months ago did this take place?"

"Twenty-eight."

"And who was the donor?"

"Matthew Jantzen."

"So the defendant donated blood at the hospital where Tina Welker worked?"

"Yes."

"Was the blood irradiated?"

She looks at the document. "Yes."

"In the specific department in which Tina Welker worked?"

"Yes."

"Ms. Lawson, when someone donates blood for a sick friend, does that blood necessarily go to that friend?"

"No, the type might be wrong. It goes to build up the supply; donors are told and understand that."

"Does the hospital keep records of who receives a particular donor's blood?"

"Yes."

"Did I ask you to look up who received Matt Jantzen's blood?"

"Yes."

"What did you find out?"

"There is no record of anyone having received it."

"Thank you. No further questions."

Steinkamp's cross is quick and to the point.

"Ms. Lawson, was there any evidence that Tina Welker tampered with or stole any of the donated blood?"

"I have no idea. I certainly didn't look for any evidence like that back then. That wouldn't be my responsibility."

"Are there significant precautions taken to protect the blood and keep it sterile and safe?"

"Certainly."

"Thank you."

aptain Dustin Oliver once again sits on the witness stand.

"Well, Captain, this is getting to be something of a habit."

He nods, but does not smile. "Yes, it is."

I ask him to explain what happened on Saturday night at the hospital, and he does so. It takes about five minutes, during which I do not interrupt. His rendition is concise but compelling; I suspect he has rehearsed it.

Unfortunately, as has been the problem all along, none of it is necessarily connected to the Welker and Charkin murders.

When he's finished, I ask, "Did you and I speak after all this?"

"Yes."

"What did I tell you?"

"That you had interviewed Michael Mitchell at the jail, and—"

Steinkamp jumps out of his chair to object that what is about to take place is inadmissible hearsay. I knew it was coming and am surprised it took Steinkamp as long as he did to lodge the objection.

He requests a conference outside the presence of the jury. Judge Pressley agrees and tells Steinkamp and me to come back to her chambers.

When we get seated, the court reporter is there to take down everything that is said. Judge Pressley asks Steinkamp to go first, which he seems eager to do.

"Your Honor, this is not hearsay, this is double hearsay. Mitchell told it to Carpenter and Carpenter told it to Captain Oliver. How can Oliver possibly quote Mitchell to this jury?"

The judge turns to me. "Mr. Carpenter, is it actually your position that this is not hearsay?"

"It definitely is hearsay, Your Honor. Mr. Steinkamp is right about that."

Steinkamp jumps in. "And it does not qualify under any of the hearsay exceptions. Had Mr. Carpenter taped the conversation with Mitchell, it would be admissible because Mitchell obviously cannot be here to testify himself. But that is clearly not what happened here."

"It does qualify as an exception, Your Honor. As I'm sure you know, even if Mr. Steinkamp seems not to, there is a catchall hearsay exception."

"Oh, come on . . . ," Steinkamp says, which I don't think is an actual legal argument, at least not in New Jersey and New York, where I practice.

"For the record, I'd like to list the relevant requirements for the catchall exception." I glance at the court reporter. "One is that the testimony is likely to be trustworthy. Captain Oliver clearly has no reason to lie, and I would have gained nothing by lying to him, unless I somehow knew that Mr. Mitchell was going to die the next day.

"Two, the testimony is offered to prove a material fact. Three, it will further the cause of justice. If Captain Oliver is allowed to testify, you will clearly see that those two conditions have been met. If they are not, you can disallow the testimony, tell the jury to disregard, hold me in contempt, and prohibit me from ever having another lobster roll."

"I think I would take some pleasure in that, Mr. Carpenter," the judge says. "I'll allow the testimony, but will cut it off quickly if I don't like what I'm hearing."

I thought that is what she would do, but I was still nervous about it. The argument was a close call, but my assumption was that the judge would not be inclined to take a key defense witness away, especially since that would invite a potential overturn on appeal.

When we get back into court, Oliver resumes his position on the stand. "Captain, you were describing what I said to you about my conversation with Mr. Mitchell in the jail."

Oliver nods. "Right. You told me that he said Henry Stokan killed Tina Welker. That he did it because Ms. Welker had found out about the plot to steal the cesium and was going to the FBI with that information. The murders were to silence her. Peter Charkin was there and was killed at the same time to keep him quiet as well."

"Why are you testifying to this? Why is Mr. Mitchell not here testifying himself?"

"He was found hanged in his cell yesterday."

I let Oliver off the stand and say five of the scariest words in the English language:

"Your Honor, the defense rests."

Steinkamp's closing argument is short and to the point.

He tells the jury that while they have been listening to some fascinating storytelling, there has been no substance behind it.

"Here's the bottom line. Matthew Jantzen's blood was found at the scene of the crime, literally on the victim's hand. Mr. Carpenter would have you believe he was framed, that the real killers chose to blame the crime on someone they never knew or heard of.

"Does that make sense? What if Matthew Jantzen had an alibi for that night? What if he was having dinner with the governor?"

"There is no evidence that Mr. Jantzen's blood was stolen. None. But there is plenty of evidence he was in that house that night."

I decide to make my closing short as well. We are really arguing over one thing, and I feel like I have the upper hand. I don't want to obscure it with extraneous stuff.

"Ladies and gentlemen, this trial started with Mr. Steinkamp's opening argument. As part of that, he said, and I quote, 'The DNA is really all you need to know.'

"The prosecution's entire case was based on DNA; if not for

that, Mr. Jantzen would not be sitting here today, on trial for his freedom. If his blood was on the scene, on the victim's hand, he had to be guilty. After all, how did it get there if he was not guilty?

"I don't mind saying that I was worried about it, for a long time. I believed in Mr. Jantzen, but I did not know how to get you to believe in him, because I just didn't know how the blood got there."

"But we found out how. The testimony of Ginny Lawson and Captain Oliver makes it very clear. His blood was stolen and used to frame him. We know who stole it. It was one of the victims, who had no idea it would help her killers cover up their role.

"Judge Pressley will talk to you about reasonable doubt. Can you say with any certainty that it didn't take place as Ms. Lawson and Captain Oliver described it? Is their explanation not a reasonable one?

"The only question at issue during this trial was how did the blood get there. Now you know. And now you know that Mr. Jantzen deserved none of this. He has been sitting in jail all of this time for donating blood for a dying friend, and for saving an abused dog.

"Please send him home with our thanks."

actually think we are going to win this one.

That's a major departure from the norm for me. Usually I am positive we are going to lose; on some level I think my pessimism is good luck.

I simply think it is reasonable for a juror to at least have a reasonable doubt as to Matt's guilt. The DNA was the mountain we had to climb, and I think we vaulted over it.

If I was on the jury, that would have been game, set, and match.

That's not to say I am worry-free. I read about a theory in politics that might apply here. People develop a worldview, and when new facts come in, they adapt them to that view. If they can't do so, if they can't fit the new fact into their existing belief, then they just reject it out of hand.

That's what scares me. I think the jury spent the entire trial prepared to convict; they needed an explanation for Matt's blood being on the scene, and they weren't getting one. So they thought he was guilty. Then the explanation came along at the last minute, and I fear they might just reject it as not fitting in with their predisposition.

This has the potential to be a great week. We are supposed to pick Ricky up at camp tomorrow; I am stunned at how much I miss him. If the jury hasn't come back by then, Laurie will have to go down there alone, because I am required to stay within an hour of the courtroom in case a verdict is reached.

I can't do my normal superstitions because we're not in Paterson. For example, usually during a jury verdict wait I go to Patsy's for pizza. Unfortunately, Patsy's is currently seven hours away.

I think I want a quick jury verdict this time; that reflects my confidence. Not that I am verbalizing that confidence to Laurie or anyone else; that is a superstition no-no.

I visit Matt at the jail, and as I expected, he asks me my prediction. I don't tell him the truth; I blab something about how unpredictable juries are. Which they are.

"I think we're going to win. You were amazing."

Clearly I can't argue with that.

As I'm getting ready to leave, the door opens. It's a guard, and with him is Charlie Tilton.

"They have a verdict."

Matt looks at me. "Is that good news or bad that it came so fast?"

"One or the other. One or the other."

Matt turns to Charlie, who says, "I agree with Andy."

t is impossible for there to exist on this planet a more nervous time than waiting for a jury to give its verdict.

Everything moves in slow motion. The arrival of the judge, the jury filing in, the handing of the verdict to the clerk . . . each event takes a month to transpire.

I feel like I lose a year of my life to stress every time, and I'm not the one facing prison. I simply do not know how defendants survive it.

Matt seems more calm than most; certainly more calm than me. I can also see the anxiety in Charlie's face; he initially wanted no part of this, but he has bought in big-time. The gallery is full; this has been a big deal locally from the start, and that hasn't changed at all.

Judge Pressley tells us to stand for the clerk to read the verdict. As we do, Matt whispers, "I can't feel my legs."

I look down. "They're there."

I put my arm on his shoulder, which is my lucky pose. Charlie puts his arm on Matt's other shoulder, and we gear ourselves for what we are going to hear.

"We the jury, in the case of the *State of Maine versus Matthew Jantzen,* as to count one, the homicide of Ms. Tina Welker, find the defendant, Matthew Jantzen, not guilty of the crime of murder in the first degree."

The clerk reads the second count, but I don't think anyone hears it, including me. There is no way they could convict on one and not the other, and they don't.

The gallery explodes, which in Maine is much more restrained than a New Jersey explosion. Or New York. Or wherever.

"My God, you did it," Matt says, and hugs me and Charlie. I turn and see Laurie beaming at me. Next to her is Matt's sister, Mary Patrick, who is in full-blown sobbing mode.

George Steinkamp comes over and offers his hand. "Congratulations. You did a hell of a job, and justice was probably served."

I nod. "Good when it turns out that way."

"Come back anytime." He smiles. "But come for a vacation, not to practice law."

Picking Ricky up at camp today was fantastic. When we first saw him, he was about a hundred yards away.

He ran that distance toward us, and I think Laurie and I were both wondering who he would run to and hug first.

Spoiler alert: it wasn't me.

But I was second, and it was damn good.

We brought the dogs with us, and Ricky does a double take when he sees Hunter. "We got another dog?"

"It's a long story," Laurie says.

We head back north because we have a victory party planned for tonight at the hotel. In addition to our family of three humans and three dogs, Marcus, Corey, Sam, and Simon Garfunkel are here, as are Matt, Mary Patrick and her husband, and Charlie Tilton.

Matt is staying with the Patricks, so fortunately I didn't have to take another suite.

It turns out that King Eider's also runs Stone Cove Catering, and they provide the food. At my request it includes lobster rolls, since I've got a hunch I won't be having one for a while.

"Man, I wouldn't have missed this for the world," Charlie says.

"You were a worthy partner."

"What was said in court that day that tipped you off?"

"When you were questioning our expert, she talked about irradiating blood degrading DNA. It just all clicked into place. And Nichols had said the militia was looking to detonate a 'significant device.' I knew he must have meant a dirty bomb, and that cesium was what they needed. But I wasn't positive until Mitchell confirmed everything.

"Well, you can come up here and try a case anytime. New York is lucky to have you."

I don't bother to correct him; I surrender.

Mary Patrick and her husband come over and she hands me a check. I look at it; it's for $1,000. "It's a start," she says. "We'll be sending you seventy-five dollars a week, as promised."

"No, you won't." I hand her back the check. "I was here on vacation."

"Enjoy your brother," Laurie says. "You guys make a wonderful family."

Matt comes over while they are with us and hugs me again. Courtroom hugs are one thing; party hugs I'm not crazy about. But I don't fight it, and it's over quickly.

"I owe everything to you and him," Matt says, pointing to Hunter.

"About that," Laurie says. "We were going to offer him to you, but he loves Tara so much that we can't separate them. I hope you understand."

Matt smiles. "Totally. I'll be heading to the shelter tomorrow to get one of my own.

DAVID ROSENFELT is the Edgar Award–nominated and Shamus Award–winning author of more than twenty Andy Carpenter novels, most recently *Holy Chow*; nine stand-alone thrillers; two nonfiction titles; and three K Team novels, a new series featuring some of the characters from the Andy Carpenter series. After years of living in California, he and his wife moved to Maine with twenty-five of the four thousand dogs they have rescued.

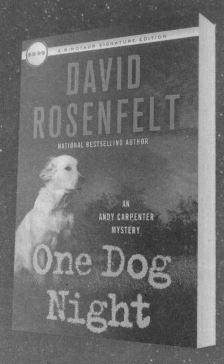